THE
COND⬤M
AND OTHER STORIES

To Eloner,
I hope you enjoy the
stories

PETER CHIKA

October 12, 2022

"A Great Goat" has previously been published in *Dear Leader Tales*, edited by E.E. King and Dan Kalin (Feral Cat, 2020). An excerpt from "Martyr" was published in *Tunnel of Lost Stories,* edited by Ruchi Acharya (Wingless Dreamer, 2020). "Headstrong" is a tongue-in-cheek reply—clapback—to "Birdsong," a short story by Chimamanda Adichie in *The New Yorker*, September 20, 2010.

Distribution by Bublish, Inc.
Published by Akikiro

ISBN: 978-1-7379634-0-0 (Paperback)
ISBN: 978-1-7379634-1-7 (eBook)

To my beloved mother, Julie Obiageli Ntephe.
Continue to rest in peace, Mom.

CONTENTS

THE CONDOM

3:35 p.m.

Ike glowered at his phone. He wanted—no *needed*—to wreak violence. Throwing a mobile phone against the wall was not it, particularly given the prices these days. He craved the old desk telephones, those hardy things whose receivers could be slammed. Even smashing them against the wall carried little consequence. There were no stored numbers to be retrieved or downloads to be restored. Or pesky phone companies to be called, for that matter. And they did not cost a small fortune. On such considerations was the mobile phone on his table safe, at least for the time being. Still, a wave of anguish swept over him. He stood up and paced his office, pounding fist into palm. All this, he thought, all this because of a condom, a stupid condom.

7:35 a.m.

Ike saw the condom at the same time as Laura did. He had just finished his ritual, morning call to Mama and was launching himself out of bed as his wife emerged from the bathroom. She was made-up and ready to go to work, her fragrance filling the bedroom. Then she froze. And he froze. For there it was. An unopened condom. On the floor. By their tangled heap of clothes from the night before.

Laura always rose before Ike. She was very orderly and ensured that their house was spick and span, with one exception. On the mornings after their frenzied trysts, she made it a point of duty to leave their clothes where they lay, as a testimonial of sorts to the continuing spontaneity of their sex. She and Ike never used condoms. Laura was Catholic. The pope forbade condoms, and that was that. For all her worldliness otherwise, and to Ike's bemusement, Laura would not compromise. They would not use condoms in their marriage.

Ike had his dalliances—he was a virile man after all, he told himself in justification. Sex with one woman would never be enough. He loved Laura with all his heart and had extraordinary sex with her but "playing away" from time to time pandered to a primordial male need for variety. Or so his rationalisation went.

There was nothing to the extramarital liaisons. They were purely physical, and he never became emotionally involved. He always bought condoms on his way to the encounters but made sure that he disposed of them, including any unused ones, at the scene of the crime. His mind now raced. How had he missed this one? How had he forgotten to throw it away? How had he been so stupid?

Ike looked from the condom to Laura. He saw her face go from disbelief to horror and then cloud with rage. She bent down ever so slowly and picked up the condom.

"Honey…" Ike started softly.

"John," she said, equally softly, straightening up and holding the condom before her.

She only called him John, his middle name, when she was upset.

"Honey," Ike pleaded, his hands suppliant. He took a step towards her.

"Don't you dare!" Laura shrieked. "Don't you dare come near me!"

"Honey…"

"Don't you 'honey' me!" Laura was near hysterical now.

Ike knew when to back off.

Laura looked as if she were about to burst into tears. Her lips twitched, but no further words came. She looked around frantically and grabbed her bag. Eyes flared, she stopped to wag a finger at Ike before storming out of the bedroom, slamming the door. She still had the condom.

Ike peered out of the window until he saw her emerge downstairs onto the road. She had taken some time to compose herself. She waved at their neighbour, pulled faces at a little girl being walked to school and headed down laughing towards the bus stop. He knew her too well. The cheery countenance belied a smouldering volcano. Despite the distance, he could make out a steely glint in her eyes. Ike John Amadi, solicitor, Taurean and number one Arsenal fan, was in trouble.

10:45 a.m.

Ike got to his office late. His mood was not helped by the rain through which he had trudged from Bank station. Even for a London morning in autumn, it was especially cold and grey. And miserably wet. The dour gods of English weather must have felt as grouchy as he did that morning. He chuckled at the thought despite his mood. Risking water damage to his phone, he had tried to call Laura as soon as he got out of the station, but the call went straight to voicemail. It would not be the only time that day he was tempted to hurl the phone.

Ike shed his raincoat and settled into his seat, having made himself a strong brew. He tried to throw himself into work, going through an agreement on his table and firing off emails. After half an hour, he admitted defeat and pushed back from the table. He moped at the window, his untouched coffee now tepid. It was still raining steadily outside. His thoughts were filled with Laura, wandering between the events of that morning and their life together.

"Excuse me," the voice said with palpable agitation. Ike raised his head, reverie broken. He was in the John Lewis store on Oxford Street, considering which television to buy for the start of the football season the next weekend. Arsenal were the reigning champions, and Ike wanted to watch them defend their title in the latest technology. He had closed work early to give himself enough time to browse the choices.

"Were you talking to me?" he asked the blonde woman who was looking at him from the next aisle.

"Yes," the woman said. "Can you come over here?" It was not a request.

Ike comprehended immediately. A dark-suited black man in a high-end, central London shop could only mean one thing. He suppressed a smile and went over. Standing before her, he could not help but think that she was the most beautiful woman he had seen in a long time. Whatever perfume she had on smelt like heaven.

"Does this come in another colour?" she demanded.

"Like what colour?" Ike responded.

"Like shocking pink?" she said.

"I really don't know," Ike said, looking directly at her. "Perhaps we should ask someone who actually works here."

The woman's eyes widened in realisation. She started to say something, but Ike stopped her with a wave of the hand and shake of the head. He caught the attention of a shop assistant, whom he beckoned over. As the assistant took charge with predictable obsequiousness, Ike went back to his televisions.

He was deep in contemplation on product specifications when he sensed a tentative presence beside him. He looked up to see the beautiful blonde woman, her face now a picture of mortification.

"I'm really sorry, sir, but I wanted to apologise for what happened a few minutes ago. It's just that..."

"The suit confused you?" Ike completed. As the woman blushed, Ike broke into a wide grin and offered his hand. "Don't mind me. My name's Ike, and I think you are the most beautiful woman who's ever mistaken me for a security guard."

She grinned back at him, looking relieved, and shook his hand. "My name's Laura and I think you are the most handsome man I've ever mistaken for a security guard."

They both laughed. She offered to buy him coffee and he accepted, his televisions and football instantly forgotten. Coffee would turn to dinner and then to late drinks at a bar in Mayfair. By the time they parted at the Bond Street station, Ike was smitten.

Laura was a riot. She had a self-deprecating sense of humour which he thought unusual for a woman so beautiful. She loved Caribbean culture and had chosen to live in Brixton where she could be surrounded by its purveyors. From time to time, she would break into Jamaican patois to relate what some dreadlocked man or the other had said to her in Brixton Market. She had a master's degree from

University College London, specialising in mid-twentieth-century feminist literature, and taught at the prestigious Dulwich College in south London.

1:00 p.m.

Ike tried Laura again. Her phone still went to voicemail. They always spoke at lunchtime, no matter how busy either of them was. She was making him stew on purpose, or worse, she was so furious that she could not trust herself to speak to him. Ike suspected it was the latter. He considered calling Tina, Laura's friend who also taught at Dulwich, but dismissed the thought. Instead, he went downstairs to buy a sandwich, only to find that he had no appetite. He stood for a bit in front of the shop, watching Londoners go about their business hunched up against the dripping rain. All the while, he thought about Laura. He did not know what he would to say to her if she answered the phone. For the umpteenth time that day, he wondered at that condom. How could he have been so careless as to leave it in his trousers?

Ike and Laura first made love two weeks after they had met, in her flat. Ike's infatuation with women usually ended as soon as he had sex with them. He likened it to Adam's eyes opening in the Garden of Eden. Once the forbidden fruit was partaken of, it did not seem quite so attractive anymore. With Laura, things were different. For the first time he could remember, Ike was besotted post-coitus.

The sex had been mind-blowing. Laura was skilled and assertive, adept at giving and taking pleasure in bed. She had a plethora of toys and lubricants, was given to manoeuvring into all sorts of impossible positions and talked suitably dirty throughout. They made love many times, every day, for the next week, and she moved in with him a fortnight later. They were married by the end of the year.

Ike considered himself an accomplished lover, but it was not difficult for him to accept that his technique improved a lot under Laura's insistent tutelage. No more evident was this than when he first cheated on her, three months after their wedding.

It was a one-night stand with Joan, a woman he met in the pub one Saturday, when Laura travelled to France on a school trip. As he climaxed, he shouted out Laura's name, much to his subsequent embarrassment. Rather than being affronted, Joan expressed gratitude. "Whoever Laura is," she said, "thank her loads for me, luv—she's the one behind the best sex I've ever had, innit?"

The experience with Joan provoked a spiral of infidelity. The sex never came close to that which he continued to enjoy with Laura, but it gave him a different kind of pleasure. Primal need for sexual variety and all that, yes, but there was more. The plaudits Ike now invariably received after the fact from the women pandered to his ego and increased his appetite for more conquests.

Most importantly, he got an intoxicating thrill—even if he would not admit it—from the danger in cheating on Laura. Laura could not stand infidelity and, especially with her abhorrence of condoms, thought it not far removed from the end of the world. He had no doubt that she would immediately leave him if she had the slightest clue that he was unfaithful. He could not bear the thought of life without her.

7:00 p.m.

Ike stood at their front door. He still did not know what he was going to say, but it was time to get it over with. It had been the worst day of his life. Taking a deep breath, he turned the key in the lock. Laura was sitting at the dining table, looking morose. Ike sat opposite her wearily and started, "Laura…"

She cut him off. Her voice was surprisingly soft. "Honey, marriage is about trust."

"I know but…" Ike said.

"Let me finish," she said in a stronger voice. "Without trust, darling, we have nothing. Absolutely nothing."

Ike's heart sank.

Laura continued. "If you wanted us to do the birth control thing, all you had to do was tell me. We could have talked about it. Catholicism will not come between us and a happy marriage. I know you don't want children yet; that's fine. Neither do I, and you know that."

Ike could not believe what he was hearing.

"I felt betrayed that you would consider using a condom with me—perhaps you've even done so—without telling me. No, darling. We talk about things, and we compromise. I was hurt in the morning, but I thought about it all day. I realised that the trust I want means that I too have to talk to you about what I don't like."

"And?" Ike asked.

"And I don't like my baby not talking to me about wanting us to use condoms. So let's talk, darling. Let's talk now about us and using condoms in our marriage."

Ike reached over and kissed his wife, waves of relief washing over him.

1:16 p.m.

Laura and Tina sat in a Starbucks in Dulwich village.

"Have you decided what to do?" Tina asked over her latte.

"Yes, Tina, I have a plan. I still don't know how I forgot the bloody condom in my jeans. I always leave them at Steve's place. I've never been as shocked as when I saw that condom this morning. And then I saw the look of guilt on Ike's face."

"But how did you know the condom was yours?" Tina pressed.

"It was a nonlatex condom, Tina. Latex gives me severe irritation down there. Steve introduced me to nonlatex. That's why I picked it up as quickly as I could. If Ike had looked closely, he might have realised it wasn't his. Or then again, men being men, he might not have!"

"Oh, the poor darling," Tina laughed. "But you can't let him off the hook?"

"Like I said, babe, this here is a woman with a plan."

The two women high-fived and laughed some more.

THE WAGER

It was just after the lunch hour. The poorly ventilated auditorium of the law faculty was dark and stuffy, as usual. The creaking ceiling fans were doing little more than circulating the warm air, as usual. The final-year class was paying rapt attention to Professor Okeke, as usual. And then, quite unexpectedly, the unusual happened.

A hum arose, the class turning from Prof towards the door. There, framed against the doorway by the blazing sun, was the statuesque figure of Yvonne Oki. One slender arm cradled her books against her bosom and the other gripped the strap of the trendy bag slung over her shoulder. She peered into the auditorium before deliberately reaching inside the bag to deliberately bring out her phone which she deliberately switched off. A chill swept through her seated classmates despite the weather. The most beautiful girl in the law faculty could not have suddenly taken leave of her senses, could she? Surely, she could not be planning to walk into Prof's class mid-lecture, could she?

Professor Okeke taught jurisprudence, a compulsory course which had to be passed for the bachelor's degree. It was already difficult enough—an "abstract" course the students called it—filled with obscurant musings about law, mostly by white men who were mostly long dead. It did not matter to the students that one of the most notable of those men, St Augustine, was African—he was as bad as the rest with all his difficult philosophising about eternal and natural law.

The students would have hated jurisprudence whoever taught it, but Professor Okeke had elevated the experience to a form of torture. It was common knowledge that he'd initially trained to be a Catholic priest in France. The truncated stint at the seminary bestowed him with fluency in not only French but also Latin. He would conjugate jurisprudence's big words in the one language and then in the other before asking the random student to explain the relevant terms, albeit in English.

The staccato questioning would start about halfway through the lecture and continue for the rest of it. Petrified students squirmed in their seats as this modern-day Torquemada trudged up and down the aisles, each hoping not to be the next unfortunate fixed with his bespectacled glare and the dreaded "You, sir, would you explain…" It was always "sir," whatever the gender of the student for, as all knew, Prof considered that there were no women at the Bar.

"Have you ever seen him ask me a question?" Yvonne asked George. Yvonne and George were cousins and hung out regularly on campus. This night, they were seated at the "Base," a bush bar behind the women's hall of residence. George was lamenting how Prof had destroyed him earlier that day with some unfathomable question about Plato.

"What do I care about Plato? The man has been dead for over a million years, abeg."

Yvonne laughed. "But Georgie," she said, placing the emphasis on the second syllable so it came out as *jhor-JHEE*, "you should have seen yourself. We think say you want shit for trouser."

"Abeg, leave me hand," George retorted, matching her switch to Pidgin English. "We dey wait, one day it will be your turn."

"But that's what I'm trying tell you now," Yvonne exclaimed, "it won't happen!"

"And why do you say so?" George asked. "That prof is no respecter of persons, I swear. He seems to enjoy picking on the hot babes especially."

With a twinkle in her eye, Yvonne affirmed, "I'm telling you, it just won't happen—not to this babe at least."

She raised her hands above her head and shook herself from side to side, laughing excitedly, like one celebrating a victory.

George took a swig of his beer and spluttered, "You girls can like to deceive yourselves. Don't worry, that day will come. Just remind me not to laugh too much at you."

Yvonne's laughter receded. She seemed to mull over what she was going to say next. Then she leaned over and crooked an arm around George's neck.

"Let me tell you something, my dear bro," she said, almost whispering. "That professor of whom all of you are so afraid is dying—I say *dyyying*—for little me. He's been hitting on me, left, right and center, from day one of jurisprudence."

She waited a moment for her words to sink in and then started to laugh again, rocking from side to side, with her hand still around his neck.

"Impossible," George exclaimed, extricating himself from her grip and turning his head to regard her with a look of disbelief. "Prof? Prof? Which prof? Abeg, pull the other leg. We're not even sure that one likes women. Have you seen the way he dresses?"

Professor Okeke was always well groomed, coiffed and attired. The contrast between him and the rest of the faculty could not be starker. Where other law teachers seemed bent on living up to the stereotype of the shabbily dressed, absent-minded professor, Prof was the epitome of sartorial elegance. To all who beheld him, there could be little doubt that he had a line to Mai Atafo, the menswear stylist.

Prof forswore the black suits that were de rigueur in the law faculty. "*Noir est pour les morts,*" he had been heard to say, denouncing that most sombre of colours as only fitting for the deceased. He turned out instead in hues he deemed tropically appropriate—"*tropicis signis*"— light blues and greys, usually in cotton or linen, rarely wool. Whatever the preferred shade for the day (but never black), the suit would be beautifully tailored and set off by pristine, cotton shirts and luxuriant ties. Cufflinks, tiepins and pocket squares accessorised the haute-couture ensemble.

If Prof's lectures were on a Friday, he dressed down. The suits were replaced by unstructured jackets and chinos. Soft leather loafers supplanted the spit-polished oxfords that were weekday staples. A cravat completed the business-casual look for, as all knew, Prof's neck could not be unadorned.

The dapper academic's attention to detail did not stop at apparel. Prof's face had the sheen of a man who availed himself of the moisturisers, cleansers and other facial-care products that had inveigled their way into men's bathroom cabinets. Despite the heat, he never seemed to sweat. His full head of hair, tending towards an afro, was always trimmed and lined around the temple and at the back of his neck. He parted it left of center, in the fetching manner of Patrice Lumumba, the Congolese nationalist.

Yvonne laughed at George's wide-eyed disbelief.

"Look here, brother me, let me show you something, doubting Georgie like you."

She thrust her phone into George's hands and showed him texts from a contact named "Mugu 4." They were all soppy, lovelorn messages. There was a smattering of French and Latin phrases in many of them. One seemed to be a poem in Latin. Another reproduced lyrics from the Afrobeat song, "African Queen."

It was George's turn to laugh. He was particularly tickled by the sobriquet Yvonne had assigned to the sender of the messages. "*Mugu*"—someone prone to deception, the moniker much beloved of 419 scammers.

"How many *mugus* exactly do you have on this phone? And wait, am I also *mugu*-something?" George chortled as he made to access her contacts list.

Yvonne snatched her phone back, laughing. "Come on, give me my phone!"

"But that proves nothing, *sha*," George asserted, drinking more beer. "The mugu fit be anybody, even one of our classmates trying to flex like Prof."

Yvonne shrugged, "Prove what? I've told you, if you don't believe me, that's your business."

George set down his bottle. He leaned forwards, resting his elbows on his lap and interlocking his fingers.

"Ivonime, Ivonime, Ivonime. How many times have I called you? Abeg, *fashi*—Professor Okeke does not chase women talk less of a student like you, as fine as you be. You hear me? He does not chase women."

Yvonne's name was really Ivonime. Like all "woke" babes on campus, she had anglicised it. You could not be woke and have some bush, native name, like some *mgbeke* from the village.

Yvonne, a certified, thoroughly woke babe, now felt challenged.

"You've called me three times, Georgie, and it is three times too many. Look, seriously, do you want to bet on this thing?"

Thus it came to be that Yvonne was standing conspicuously outside the auditorium well after Prof's class had started on this hot afternoon. It had not taken any stretch of the imagination for the cousins to arrive at an appropriate wager. Professor Okeke was a punctilious timekeeper. He started his classes on the dot of the hour and finished similarly. He did not tolerate lateness.

In one oft-recounted incident, a class preceding Prof's had overrun in another lecture hall. The students coming from that class arrived at the auditorium to find that Prof was already ten minutes into his lecture. He broke off only long enough to give the gaggle congregating at the door a stern warning not to attempt ingress. The incredulous students were therefore forced to stand outside taking notes as best they could as Prof finished an hour's lecture to a vacant auditorium. He even walked the empty aisles from the half-hour mark, although it was the only time anyone could remember that the dreaded "And you, sir…" was not part of the exercise.

Now, with all eyes fixed on her, Yvonne dramatically stepped into the auditorium. Her pace was measured, heels clicking and clacking in the pin-drop silence, as her peers watched with trepidation. Prof had stopped teaching. Yvonne was now in the firing line. Surely, an explosion was coming. Or was it?

Yvonne got to the front of the lectern and paused, her back to the professor. She surveyed the ascending rows for an empty seat. She seemed oblivious to the immaculately attired figure behind her who stood wordless at the lectern, his designer glasses glinting and an odd, strangled look on his face.

After a seeming eternity, Yvonne espied a spot at the top of the auditorium and began to make her way up slowly. She had chosen a seat in the middle of an occupied row. Students had to get up, moving bags, laptops and notepads, to let her through. The seat bottoms swished up, thudding against backrests as the row progressively rose for Yvonne. It was a commotion most unbecoming of the jurisprudence hour. Yet, Prof stood, transfixed, saying nothing and doing nothing.

Eventually, Yvonne got to her preferred seat. She made another deliberate show of bringing out her books and gathering her weave at the back of her head with a band. The students cast astonished, if furtive, glances from Prof to Yvonne. Still nothing happened. There was no explosion, no multilingual rant, nothing, not a word from Prof. Yvonne sat, silence reigning once more, with notebook open, pen poised in hand.

And then, like one emerging abruptly from a trance, Prof resumed his lecture.

"As we shall see, critical legal studies were preceded by the realist school whose main proponent was Oliver Wendell Holmes Jr."

The students were jolted back to their note taking.

That day, for the first time in living memory, Professor Okeke did not venture up the aisles. He did not ask anybody any questions. He did not speak any French or Latin. He also finished his lecture a full ten minutes before time and was sweating profusely by the end.

After Professor Okeke departed, uncharacteristically mopping his brow, if with a monogrammed handkerchief, it was an animated final-year law class that spilled out of the auditorium. They were full of excited chatter, trying to comprehend what had just happened. All bar two. That night, George handed over one thousand naira to Yvonne. She graciously used some of it to buy him beer.

THE BRIEFCASE

It happened at the Capital Oil filling station on Zik Avenue. As surely as it was December, that month of frantic shopping and travelling, there was a fuel scarcity. The queue to the station was at least a mile long. It was not yet gone 7:00 a.m., but some of us had been here, in the Harmattan cold, for over three hours. Those whose cars were within view of the station had mostly left them and gathered by the pumps. There our numbers were swelled by those nondescript itinerants that routinely populated the scenes of our chaos.

Cars were being let into the station in groups of six. Each time a group exited, we would rush back to our cars and inch them forward as appropriate. Then we would return to the pumps. Why did we not stay in our cars? Well, we had to know what was happening at the end of the queue. We had to be sure there was no *wuru wuru*—funny business—going on. We did not trust fuel queues, and we trusted the next person in them even less. That was how we were in this country.

Occasionally an argument would break out among us, but mostly it was just banter we carried on in that raucous manner for which we, the common people, are known. Big men and women were, of course, not here; they either sent their drivers or had special consignments delivered to them at home. It was only us, the masses, who suffered the scourge of fuel queues. That was how it was in this country.

And there we were, ordinary people at the pumps, when a sharp cry pierced the hubbub. "Stop there! Thief! *Onye ori*! I say stop there!" Our heads jerked in unison. A man in the type of outfit that we call a "safari suit" had broken from our ranks. Shouting at the top of his voice, he sprinted to another man walking away from the station and snatched at the briefcase held by the latter. A scuffle immediately ensued.

There was nothing we loved like "two fighting," as our police called incidents like this. We hastily abandoned the pumps to converge around the antagonists. "Gimme my bag, gimme my bag," raged safari-suited man. "See this man, see this man," screeched the adversary, who was shabby of attire in comparison to his assailant. "It is my bag that you are claiming! God punish you!"

Engaging in a robust tug of war over the briefcase, each grabbed the other's shirt around the collar. We called this fighting stance "*ikpo tie*" as it evoked a tie-knotting motion, albeit a decidedly unfriendly one. Once things got to that stage in two fighting, it was the bounden duty of onlookers to intervene. Some of us grabbed one man, others grabbed the other and we prised them apart. We also wrested the briefcase.

Having been physically restrained but still within a few feet of each other, the two men resorted to volleying invective while kicking out in the direction of each other.

"Thief, you are a proper thief, *onye ori*."

"Your father. God punish you."

"See this riff-raff o. Nonsense."

"Thunder fire your head. Idiot."

"You are a goat."

"Monkey."

"Bastard."

"Your mama."

And so on.

Would-be interlocutors were also talking, each trying to make himself heard by either antagonist or by the general body of people. For a few moments, it was babel. But there is a science to such commotions, and some assertive voices soon rose above the confusion, quietening us down. A thickset man with thick lips imposed himself as chief mediator. We called such dominant males "Dike" (pronounced *Dee-KAY*) as much for their physical features as their commanding presence.

"Wetin be the problem?" this Dike intoned in Pidgin English, enquiring as to the cause of contention. Our two central characters started talking at the same time. *Katakata* burst out again, but our resident Dike quickly arrested it.

"See, it will be turn by turn talking here," proclaimed Dike. Turning to Safari Suit, Dike directed, "you, sir, you go talk first."

Shabby immediately perked up, "Why him? I say why him? Because he wear good cloth? Chai, poor man have suffer in this world."

Dike immediately cut him off. "You this man! Sharrap! I say it is turn by turn now."

We nodded and murmured our agreement with Dike, a few of us assuring Shabby that he would get his opportunity. "Cool down, you too will get chance to talk."

Dike turned to Safari Suit again. "*Oga*," he said, using the deferential term by which we addressed important people around here, "what is the problem?"

Safari Suit freed himself from his restrainers, deliberately adjusted his jacket around the collar and spoke up. "This man is a thief. *Onye ori.*"

"*Na* you be thief," came the retort from Shabby before the crowd hushed him again.

Safari Suit continued. "I have been here at this station since morning. You all saw me. I was here at the pump when I saw this good-for-nothing man putting his dirty, stinking hand into my car and taking my briefcase. Then he started walking away as if nothing. If not for God, I would not have seen him, but my God is alive, and I saw him. God has caught him today. I just want my briefcase back. It is God that will punish him."

Dike sought clarification that Safari Suit was claiming ownership, "So therefore, you say *na* you get this bag?"

"Of course, it is mine," confirmed Safari Suit. "Does this useless riff-raff look like someone who can afford a briefcase like this?"

Some of us laughed. The briefcase did indeed look beyond Shabby's means if appearances were anything to go by.

Shabby let out a wail. "I have suffered. So poor man cannot fit to hold briefcase again? Chai, I have suffered."

There was more laughter.

Dike then turned to Shabby. "You hear the thing this gentleman talk, *abi*? *Wetin* you talk?"

Shabby began, in halting English. "See me o. I be jobseeker o. Jobseeker. It is interview I am going o."

We had a habit of adding the odd "o" at the end of sentences for emphasis. This inflection was particularly pronounced when we were agitated. Shabby was naturally in a state of high agitation. He was also gesticulating wildly, as we tended to do in such circumstances.

"I am just walking on my own. Suddenly, I am shock to see this animal from nowhere coming to call me thief. And insult upon injury, he is struggling my bag. My own bag o. My bag. To God, I never know say thief for this our country has reach like this where they can disguise in suit like this...this...devil."

Emphasising that the briefcase was his, Shabby finished his declamation with one of our beloved exclamations, "*Tufia*!" and spat in the direction of Safari Suit. At this, Safari Suit, who had been snorting derisively, made for Shabby. Both had to be restrained again.

Our Dike then spoke up. "So you say the bag is your own, and you too say is your own?" Both men nodded vigorously, shooting dangerous looks at each other.

"You, what is your name?" Dike continued.

Safari Suit said, "Chudi. Chudi Okafor."

"And you, what is your name?"

"Emeka Agu," Shabby answered.

"Okay, let me see," Dike said, hefting the briefcase to examine it. "No name or anything like that on top this bag o." Dike showed the briefcase around the circle that we constituted, and we concurred that there was no name tag or anything like that on it.

"So how we can know who get this bag now?" Dike asked, almost rhetorically. He tried to open the briefcase, but it was firmly locked.

"The person who owns that bag must have the key," said one of us.

"Yes o," the rest of us chorused, acknowledging the wisdom of the bright spark.

Dike now looked to the two combatants. "Okay o, the one that bring key, we know that it is him that own this bag."

Each man immediately started checking his pockets and patting himself down as men do when looking for keys. Neither seemed able to find the requisite key, much to our mirth. Dike spoke up again. "See this people o? Nobody can find the key."

"I'm sure it must be in my car," Safari Suit said. "Let me go and find it."

A few of us followed him to his car. He rummaged around the glove compartment—or "pigeonhole" as we knew it. He checked by the gearbox. He looked under the seats. He raised the floor mats. He put his hands between the seats. After this searching "up and down" as we described that kind of thorough search, he acknowledged defeat with a puzzled look on his face. He stood still for a moment, brows furrowed in contemplation, hands akimbo. Then he shook his head and raised his hands in surrender. We all proceeded back to where the rest waited.

"So it is not in your car," Dike growled.

"No," Safari Suit said. "I don't...wait o, okay, I know what to do! My house is not far from here. I can just drive there and get the spare key. It won't take me ten minutes and I'll be back."

Shabby, who had been smiling to himself since, now spoke up. "For where? You will go to where? So that you can run away? You and me will stay here o. Come has come to become and you want to disappear? *Wuru wuru* man. God have catch you today."

Another round of abuse ensued between the antagonists. Ignoring them, Dike conferred with a few of us and turned to Shabby, "You, where you live?" Shabby said he lived far away in Udi, a sleepy village at least an hour away from where we were. The spare key was under his bed in his room in Udi, he said. Dike conferred again. Our consensus was that since Safari Suit said he lived nearby, we should let him go to see if he could get the spare key.

When Dike pronounced our decision, Safari Suit smiled broadly at us and shook Dike's hand. He straightened his clothes again, glowered once more at Shabby and said, "You just wait, you good-for-nothing criminal, you must sleep in police cell tonight."

"*Yeye* man," Shabby jeered. "You will chop shame today. It is you that God will use to prove that the devil is a big liar."

As Safari Suit departed, he turned to us, "Don't let him run away o. I'm coming back in the next ten minutes. My house is just behind here." And then he was gone, confidently manoeuvring his car out of the queue, executing a U-turn, and roaring off.

We waited. Ten minutes became thirty and then one hour and then more. There was no sign of Safari Suit. Many of us in the original crowd drifted away, the matter having lost its moment. The queue had moved considerably. Many of the first interlocutors filled their tanks and drove away to the business of the day, whatever it was for them. The itinerants too had tired of this filling station, perhaps because the queue was too orderly for their liking. Only a few of us elected to remain to see things to the end. Dike was one of us stragglers. He was clearly enjoying his prolonged fifteen minutes of authority.

At first, Shabby had been content to sing to himself with a wry smile on his face. As time wore on though, he became increasingly insistent. "I told you o. I told all of you o. Okay now, where is he? I say where is he now? Where? Where o?" We initially bid him to be quiet. The more time passed, however, the stronger he railed and the weaker our assertions that he "exercise patience."

Eventually, even Dike tired of waiting. The sun had risen high in the sky, dispelling the morning cold. The heat was becoming unbearable and the premises offered scant shade. Rearing himself to his full height, Dike announced, "True, true, it is like that man has run away o. Wonders will never cease in this our country."

The rest of us rose from the ground where we had been sitting around Shabby and dusted off the seats of our trousers. We executed exaggerated shrugs of the shoulder, miming wonderment at the disappearance of the seemingly trustworthy Safari Suit. Many of us clicked thumb against third finger, drawing a circle over our heads with the clicking hand as we did so.

Dike addressed us. "It is like it is this man that own the bag o," he said, pointing at Shabby. "Let us give him his bag to be going."

There was an affirmative chorus. "Yes o, yes o."

But then someone spoke up. "Even though it seems it is his bag, since we have waited like this, let us open the bag, see what is inside and see whether it is this man that owns the bag true, true. At least, if that other man should eventually come back to claim it, we will tell him to his face that he is a liar because we have seen what is inside the bag."

We looked at one another. It was indeed a wise suggestion.

Shabby made to protest. "Look, why damaging my bag now. See as the other man have run away. Just give me my bag, let me be going my way."

The seed had been sown and we said no. Either he opened the briefcase or we would force it open. Shabby pleaded some, arguing that this was a special bag given to him by his late father. He only brought out the bag for special occasions like his interview on this day. What would we gain, he asked, by destroying this one thing that his father had left for him?

We were having none of it. Unless we were not the sons of our fathers, we were going to see what was inside that briefcase. Someone volunteered a large screwdriver, and another brought a stone. Dike did the honours. Crouching and putting the screwdriver to the lock, he struck twice with the stone. The lock snapped. The circle we had formed around Dike edged closer. He looked up around deliberately and then fixed his gaze on Shabby. With a flourish, Dike flung open the lid. The next moment he was jumping back in shock.

Right there before our eyes, in the now open briefcase, wrapped in blood-soaked cellophane, were human body parts, including what looked like a man's genitals. We shouted in horror, wide-eyed. Shabby shouted too, his hands on his head. He took another look at the grisly contents and threw himself on the ground, rolling around in the dirt. This brought some of us out of our stupor and we rounded on him. He started to cry, "It is not my bag o. I swear to God. I be thief, I be common thief o. I see bag for that man car. I take the bag. The bag is not mine o. I am a thief, I be pickpocket, but I am not a killer o. I am not a ritualist. The bag is that man own. It is not my own o. Somebody help me o, please, please. Somebody help me. Chai, I am dead!"

We never knew what became of Shabby after we handed him, and his gory package, over to a passing police patrol. The last we saw of him, he was manacled and sitting on the floor in the back of their receding pickup. One of the policemen was gleefully slapping him around the head. Shabby was still loudly protesting his innocence. Who knows, perhaps he eventually had his day before a magistrate. Or perhaps he was one of those who disappeared en route to the police station, never to be seen again. That was how we were in this country.

SCENT OF A CHILD

I didn't know it was a man that my son married.

The words stung Ada as viciously as when they had first been spoken by her mother-in-law that morning. She cast a furtive glance sideways as she entered the dim corridor. She was assaulted by a rancid odour which she recognised as the commingling smells of kerosene cooking, cheap stews and unwashed bodies. The odour hung thick in the corridor as she made her way down gingerly, her eyes adjusting to the poor light.

Bits and pieces, junk in her eyes, but which she appreciated would be precious to the inhabitants of this dingy tenement, lined her way. These houses in the poorer parts of town were called "face-me-I-face-you" for their cramped conditions. Whole families lived in each of the rooms on both sides of the long corridor, eating, sleeping and eking out a miserable existence which they bore with surprising equanimity.

She had previously been to dwellings like this only when she was looking for a new housemaid. She rarely entered, and when she did, was accompanied by the driver or someone else. This time her objective made it imperative that she be alone.

The corridor opened onto a yard, crisscrossed by lines on which washing had been hung to dry. She reflected again that these clothes would be highly prized by those who lived here even if they seemed like rags to her. There were two children playing at one side of the yard. They were the first people she was encountering here today but were completely oblivious to her. She liked that. She had timed her visit for when she figured most of the adult inhabitants would be absent, pursuing the menial jobs on which their existence depended.

She stepped under the washing lines, pushing past clothes smelling faintly stale, to the back of the yard where there was a hut with a wooden door. There were goats tethered outside and a large spherical basket full of native chickens. It was precisely as had been described to her.

She paused at the door, hesitant for perhaps the first time since she'd decided to make the journey. Then she heard those words again.

A man, you hear me? I say you are nothing but a man.

She knocked on the door.

There was a cough from within and a phlegmatic voice spoke up. "Enter into the presence of those who own us."

The door creaked as she opened it, but she was pleased to see it was not dark inside. A window at the back of the hut let in sunlight so that she saw clearly the seated man with a graven expression whose eyes seemed to bore into her soul. She genuflected on impulse.

"*Nna anyi*," she said, uttering a phrase that meant "our father" but was also used as a general term of reverence for a much older man. "I greet you."

"I greet you also, my daughter," he responded in a solemn voice. "You are Erinne's friend?"

"Yes, *nna anyi*."

"I have been expecting you. She told me about you. Please sit down."

Ada gathered her *boubou* carefully before lowering herself onto one of the stools opposite him. He was sitting in an armchair with frayed upholstery, his wiry arms on the rests. She supposed the seating arrangements were purposely contrived to give him a regal bearing accentuated by the suppliant position which the stool now forced her to assume.

There was a time-worn, 1970s-style coffee table between them, the single shelf under the tabletop packed with dusty piles of old newspapers. Ada wondered again at this penchant of poor people for collecting junk. She quickly dismissed the thought, momentarily apprehensive that this impassive man might be able to read her mind.

The old man seemed to be studying her. She made to speak but he held up a hand and she kept quiet. He had on a stained singlet—the tank top pejoratively known as a "wife-beater" in America. In the context of her mission, she reflected that there was some irony in the moniker. A wrapper was knotted at his waist and flowed onto his unshod feet. She recognised it as Hollandis, that wax-printed fabric so beloved of Africans, but this looked nothing like the pristine bales in her wardrobe. This wrapper had seen so much wear and tear that she would not even consider handing it down to any of her maids.

The armchair rested against an iron-spring bed, on which was a thin mattress that was particularly depressed in its middle and covered with a filthy sheet that might have been white in another incarnation. Above the bed, on the wall, hung an assortment of goatskin bags and horns and the skull of a small animal. Ada had expected additional accoutrements and a more foreboding environment. She was relieved to be disappointed.

She could, however, smell the man. It was that smell which, in her perception, poor townspeople and almost everybody who lived in the villages had. It came from bodies on which no better embrocation than petroleum jelly had ever been used and whose underarms were not acquainted with deodorant. It was the product of continuous per-spiration in an unyielding tropical heat that was not tempered by air conditioning. The smell would be acute if he raised his arms—already nauseous, she willed him to keep them on the armrest.

It struck Ada that perhaps she was experiencing a heightened sen-sitivity to odour because she was ovulating. Erinne, who put her up to this visit, had insisted she go only during this period in her cycle. She had battled with the idea as the day came, only for her mother-in-law to launch the most strident tirade yet on that morning. Ada needed no further persuasion.

"And what have you sought out Odenigbo for, my daughter?" The old man had suddenly broken the silence.

"*Nna anyi*, but I thought..."

The old man smiled, his face softening for the first time since she came. "I know, my daughter. Trust me, Odenigbo knows what you have come for. But you are now in the presence of the gods and you must speak it to them with your own mouth."

She had prepared herself to foment aloofness. Her ambivalence about this recourse had not only returned but increased as she had surveyed the surroundings. This was a desperately poor man in des-perately poor circumstances, so how could he be of any help to her?

Surely, he could have done for himself if he could do for others? But now she heard her mother-in-law's shrill taunt once again, as if the woman were standing here in front of her.

There is no difference between you and a man! Tufia!

Ada blurted out, "*Nna anyi*, I want to bear a child!"

Odenigbo's tone was solemn. "How badly, my daughter? How badly do you want a child?"

"*Nna anyi*, my entire being wants a child. My spirit screams for a child. I want to be a complete woman, to carry a child in this womb, to nurture it and give birth to it. I want to shame all those who have mocked me, especially that witch that calls herself my husband's mother. *Nna anyi…*"

Ada burst into tears, her body heaving with sobs. The old man let her cry; he had seen this many times before. She wept for a while, the only other sound in the hut being the old man's intermittent coughing. The occasional clucking of the chickens and bleating of goats outside seemed to come from far away. Eventually, Ada regained her composure, but tears still rolled down her cheeks as she elaborated her entreaty.

"*Nna anyi*, please help me as you helped my friend. I can no longer bear the shame and pain. I have money…I brought the amount my friend said I should bring. I can bring more. I will do anything. Just let me have a child in this womb."

The old man contemplated her for a little while longer.

"Alright, my child. As I have been listening to you speak so the gods have been hearing your words. And they have also heard you cry. Give me a moment, let me commune with them."

The old man closed his eyes, raising his head slightly. His lips moved but Ada could not make out his words. He mumbled for a few minutes, sometimes raising his hands from the armrests with his palms facing upwards. She figured he was saying some kind of prayer. When the mumbling stopped, it was replaced by a series of exaggerated nods. The old man would nod three or four times, keep still for a moment, nod again several times and keep still. Eventually, he smiled and opened his eyes.

"My daughter, the gods will help you. You are one of the lucky ones. It is not all who come to the gods that find their favour. You have a good spirit, and the gods have seen that. You have not wished ill on those that mocked you; you merely want the fruit of your womb to shame them. The gods will help you."

"*Nna anyi*, thank you," said Ada, not entirely sure of what to say.

"Don't thank Odenigbo," said the old man, "I am merely a vessel for the gods."

"Then thank them for me, *nna anyi*."

"In time, my daughter, in time. Did your friend tell you what to bring?"

"Yes, *nna anyi*. It is here."

She opened her purse and brought out five hundred-dollar bills which she placed on the table. When Erinne had told her that the money must be in US dollars and not in naira, she had laughed up-roariously. "So even the local gods worship the Americans?" she'd asked. Erinne had given her a terse look before warning her against mocking the very forces that might be her last hope out of misery. Ada had stifled her laughter but chalked this request for payment in foreign currency as yet another reason why she should regard visiting the native doctor as a charade. There was probably a more scientific reason for Erinne's childbirth after years of trying, but perhaps the sooner she got this out of the way, the sooner reliance on rationality would resume in her case.

"I know what you are thinking, my daughter," the old man said, startling her. He had not touched the money.

"No, *nna anyi*, I... I..."

"Never mind, my child. Others in your position have voiced it. Money is spiritual; it is one of the most powerful forces even in the spirit world. The gods do not ask you for this money because they want to spend it. This American dollar you see, it attracts a powerful spirituality; it is the most powerful of all the currencies. When you come here with barrenness, it requires very powerful spirits to open your womb. We must use something very powerful from this world to call forth those spirits. It is why we ask for American money."

"I see, *nna anyi*," Ada answered, even if she did not fully see.

"We are ready to begin."

The old man got up, for the first time since she had been there, and reached into one of the goatskin bags. After a bit of rummaging, he brought out some *nzu*, the native chalk that attended so many *dibia* rites. He rubbed the *nzu* around one of his eyes. He stepped out of the hut and came back shortly with a cockerel and knife. He thrust the cockerel forwards.

"My daughter, this is yours. Part of your money has bought this."

A very expensive chicken then, Ada thought, but quickly chastised herself.

Odenigbo tied the bird's legs together with piece of string. He set it down on the edge of the table and, gathering the wings together, used his knees to pin them down away from the body. He plucked the feathers from the middle of the neck until there was clear skin. Holding the head with one hand, he slit the throat with a deft stroke, letting the blood spurt onto the floor as the dying chicken jerked. Ada noticed he was careful to not let the blood touch the money which was still on the table. Obviously, she reflected, even the gods did not like defaced notes.

When the chicken was still, the old man motioned Ada toward the puddle formed by the blood in the floor. "Kneel down, my daughter, and rub your hands vigorously in the blood. Quickly."

Ada did as she was told, all the time marveling at herself for going through with this.

"Now, my daughter, as you know, *Ani*, the mother earth, is our highest deity. You have given her a blood sacrifice, and she has received it as shown by the blood and dirt now on your hands. It is *inwu iyi* time—you must now take an oath."

"An oa-oath, *nna anyi*?" Ada stammered.

"Yes, my daughter. Repeat after me: I swear by this sacrifice that I shall keep secret everything I do here today."

"But what is it that you will want me to do, *nna anyi*? I can't make a blood oath if—"

The old man cut her short. "You must swear this oath if you want us to continue. But remember, even if you swear it, I cannot force you to do anything. Whatever the gods tell you to do hereafter must be done of your own free will."

Ada thought about what he'd said for a moment and considered that it made sense. No one, not least this smelly old man, was going to force her into some unpalatable rite. Then she heard her mother-in-law's voice again.

"What was the oath again, *nna anyi*?"

"I swear by this sacrifice that I shall keep secret everything I do here today."

Ada repeated the words.

"And if I shall break this *iyi*, may the oath take my life."

Ada hesitated, looking up at the old man. His gaze was unblinking. She barely whispered the last part of the oath, but the old man was satisfied.

"You can sit down, my daughter. Don't worry about your hands; you can wash them after we finish."

He took dead the chicken outside. Ada heard him call out. She assumed it must be to the children she had seen earlier in the yard. "Take this to your mother and tell her to make good stew for us tonight."

She heard the children's squeals of delight intermingled with the old man's laughter. She wondered wryly how they would react if she interrupted the family moment to remind Odenigbo that *she* had paid for the chicken, sacrifice or not. Surely, he should have asked her before appropriating it? She laughed to herself.

Staring at her mud-caked hands, Ada imagined the look of horror that would come upon her husband's face if he could see her now. Obi, who mocked the widespread belief in the supernatural, had unfortunately adopted the same attitude regarding her requests that he see a medical doctor to check his fertility.

As the months had lengthened from their wedding and she did not become pregnant, she grew convinced that the several abortions during her reckless undergraduate days had done fundamental damage. Comprehensive tests at her maternity clinic subsequently established to the contrary—there was nothing wrong with her. Still, Obi would not brook that the problem could be him. Instead, he insinuated that he might take up his mother's suggestion to prove where the difficulty lay by impregnating some village girl that his mother would gladly arrange.

Perhaps, thought Ada, she should have simply beseeched Odenigbo to do or give her something that would make Obi agree to see a real doctor. That might have been simpler than sitting here now wondering what else the old man was going to have her do. She did not have to wait long. The old man came back in. He was smiling.

"My children are happy with the gift you've given them. The gods delight in the happiness of children, you know?"

"Thank God for that," Ada responded before she could stop herself.

She waited for Odenigbo to rebuke her clear if impulsive reference to the Christian God, but he did not seem to have heard. He had turned his back to her to lock the wooden door. He reached under the bed and brought out two wooden boards which he used to block the window. The hut would have been in total darkness if not for a little light coming in from the gap between the bottom of the door and the floor.

The old man then stood before her. She instinctively held her breath.

"Come, my daughter, it is now time to do that which the gods require to put a child in your womb."

"*Nna anyi…?*"

The old man did not answer but gently took her hand and pointed to the bed. Ada's eyes widened in shock as realisation hit. She wrenched her hand away and with her other hand brushed violently over where the old man had held her. She felt soiled by his mere touch. She could not bear to think about what he was suggesting.

"*Nna anyi…?*" She queried again, her voice rising.

The old man stood silent. His hands were at his sides and he raised them slightly, turning them outwards so that his palms faced toward her. Ada was incensed; the old man was actually gesturing surprise at her reaction.

"*Nna anyi?*" She was now shouting. "You want me to…? Me? *Nna anyi?* Me? You must be mad. You and your stupid gods must be mad. Completely mad. You hear me?! *Mad*! *Tufia!*"

She burst into tears again, but this time it was out of rage. She could not believe that this smelly old man could have the cheek to suggest what he had. She made for the door and tried to open it, but it was latched shut. She wrenched frantically, screaming at the old man at the top of her voice.

"Come and open this door! Come and open this door! I say come and open this door!"

The old man contemplated her for a few seconds, then strode across the hut and undid the bolts. Ada ran out, weeping. There was a maddening swirl of thoughts in her head as she fled. The old man's smell filled her nose. She was retching as she ran. So this was what Erinne had wanted her to do? This was why Erinne had kept emphasising, "Whatever he tells you to do, do it; there is nothing he requires that you cannot do." And Erinne's twins? Those beautiful babies? Was this…?

Ada was suddenly in between the washing lines, the clothes forming a flailing and confusing maze. Ada thrashed around the garments blindly, losing her sense of direction and then her balance. She fell heavily onto ground. She lay there, weeping in anger, frustration and despair. After what seemed like a long time but could not have been more than a few minutes, she sensed a presence next to her. She looked up, expecting to see the old man, but instead saw the two children. They had their hands behind their necks, their stomachs jutting out, and stared at her in the way children did when they came across the curiosity of an adult having a breakdown.

Perhaps it was something about the children, but Ada felt a strange calm come over her. Her mother-in-law's words filled her head again, but this time there was no sting. It was as if they were a lullaby even. She stopped crying and got up, brushing off her *boubou*. She picked up her bag where it had fallen, gathering the things that had spilled from it. She made to brush off her *boubou* some more but, realising that her mud-caked hands only dirtied it, stopped. She stood erect and shook her head defiantly. She walked back to the hut and pushed open the door.

The old man was seated back in his chair. He looked up as she entered. He did not seem surprised. She closed the door behind her, this time locating and latching the bolts. She set her bag on the table. Putting her hands under the *boubou*, she reached for her panties and shimmied out of them. She walked around the table, past the old man, and climbed onto the bed. She raised the hem of the *boubou* at the front until it was at her waist. She spread her legs as the old man got up, tugging at the knot of his wrapper. She held her breath.

THE LIST

Osita watched his opponent snore. It was now well past 2:00 a.m. and Uche Emengo, the Great Iroko, was stretched out on the sofa, his expansive stomach spilling over the edge. The snoring began as a rattle somewhere in the recesses of that belly and reached a high-pitched crescendo before petering out in a low rumble. At times, it seemed from the sound that the snorer was suffocating. Osita ruminated on how that might solve the problem, if the Great Iroko expired then and there from natural causes. The decision would be wrested from the men of "timber and calibre" currently huddled in the anteroom. Osita Anumba, PhD, former university lecturer, would be the sole candidate for chairman of the Adimora local government council.

Osita would be the first to admit that it was hardship that had driven him into seeking electoral office. One did not need uncommon vision to know that the pay for lecturers was awful. For how long could he continue to eke out a living by selling lecture notes to supplement his meagre income? He was tormented by the endless sniggering and smirking of his students, particularly the girls who all had sugar daddies, many of whom were politicians and elected officials. A stint in government was the surest route to fabulous wealth in these parts— only a fool could argue with that. Osita had finally accepted that he'd been rather foolish, having railed in vain against VIPs—vagabonds in power—for years.

And so, quelling the last of his petulant demons, he'd decided to try his hand at the grassroots. He was overqualified to be a councilor, but the council chairmanship would do nicely. The way it worked, chairmen had complete control of local government funds, which meant that they could divert most of the money to their personal accounts. None of them passed up the chance. The little left—and it was very little indeed—they shared among their councilors and patrons.

The current chairman, the expansive Right Honourable Sam Okanku, Knight of Saint John, MPA (honoris causa), had campaigned for election with the slogan, "Operation Cleanup," promising to introduce accountability and good governance. He would make a show during campaign rallies of sweeping the stage with a broom as a picturesque metaphor for his mantra. Now, a few months before the expiration of his term in office, he was simply called "Cleanout" for the treatment he had meted out to the local government's coffers.

The council did nothing more than run after petty traders and subsistence farmers for taxes while waiting for windfalls from the central government. Still, the people did not revolt. Instead, like feudal serfs, they scrambled for handouts from the very people who kept them in penury. Despite the irreverent nickname that he had attracted, Cleanout was loveable rogue rather than loathed villain. Small crowds gathered outside his house every day for the cash gifts he doled out. He was easily one of the most popular men in the local government area. It was strange, but Osita had also given up on wondering about it.

The last straw for Osita had come when he'd taken up the matter, on the sidelines of an academic conference, with a well-known professor of politics. Osita had expected a lively conversation, peppered with the ideas of philosophers like Gramsci and Mazrui. To his dismay, the other man had refused to engage. "He for whom the pear has ripened, let him eat," said the political scientist. "One day, it might be your turn or my turn to eat."

Osita had been surprised at how receptive the political parties were. He'd first approached the Labour Party, which was regarded as the party of intellectuals, but quickly realised that they had no real presence in the local government area. He'd then talked with the Amalgamated Peoples' Congress, the main national opposition party. Their pitch was appealing, but he was gruffly advised by his father that a party formed by people from across the Niger could never win an election in these parts. "If you want to tie those people like a wrapper around you," the old man said, "you might as well consider yourself naked."

He had learnt the hard way to listen to his father, who always wanted him to study medicine. He'd opted for microbiology in a moment of adolescent rebellion and watched with regret as less stellar classmates went on to become affluent medical doctors.

Osita had settled on the ruling party, the Progressives Democratic Party. A combination of circumstances worked in his favour. The PDP rotated electoral offices between the six villages—or "autonomous communities" as they liked to call themselves—that made up the Adimora local government. It was the turn of his village to produce the next candidate for chairman.

The first problem was that he was not a registered member of the party. The PDP's constitution said a person had to have been a member for at least a year to be qualified for nomination. It was a despondent Osita that went to register, thinking that he had to postpone his ambitions until he was qualified.

Registration was the province of the party secretary in each electoral ward. It turned out that Osita's ward secretary was a former student of his. Edu Kaneme had heard of Osita's political intentions and was effusive about helping. He issued Osita a backdated registration card.

"B-b-but," Osita stuttered, "won't they check?"

Edu laughed. "Check what, sir? It is what I give them that they will take. Welcome to politics, sir!"

Osita suppressed his guilt. At least he had not bribed to get the backdated card.

He was now a bona fide member and eligible for the party's primaries. The next problem was money. Osita had none. It was Edu to the rescue again.

Edu took him to Chief Onwuka, the richest man and ultimate power broker in the local government area. Onwuka was barely literate but had proved an astute businessman. He had worked his way up from bus conductor to owner of the biggest transport company east of the River Niger. Everybody seeking elections from the six villages—nay, autonomous communities—approached him for money, and he gave according to how serious he judged the candidacy.

In times past, you paid your respects to a potential patron with kola nuts and palm wine. Nowadays, you went with the most expensive cognac. At Edu's urging, a nervous Osita cleared most of his savings to buy the case of XO that they now presented to Chief Onwuka, both supplicants bowing extremely low.

"So *dokinta*, you are wanting to do election; you are wanting to be our chairman, *ndeh*," Onwuka said. "You must to not go there and thief, are you hearing me?"

Osita was relieved. There were rumours that local government chairmen delivered ten percent of the council's monthly revenues to Chief Onwuka to retain his support. Onwuka's admonition against stealing flew in the face of such stories. Osita immediately warmed to this rotund millionaire.

Chief Onwuka said he liked the idea of a doctor—*dokinta*—aspiring to be the local government chairman. He lamented, without hint of irony, that uneducated people—"those who are not go school"—had dominated Adimora council elections in the past. He gave Osita five million naira in cash, for starters, to fund the campaign. Osita had never seen such money in one place before. The amount meant that Chief Onwuka thought him to be a potential election winner. Things were falling into place faster and better than he had imagined.

Edu became his campaign manager and organised his first rally. Osita researched the local government's statistics vigorously, drawing on his university connections. He prepared the kind of socialist manifesto he'd always yearned to hear, but never did, from election candidates in the country. He was going to introduce the villagers to the sort of rousing campaign speeches that CNN and BBC showed to be the norm in Western countries.

To Osita's consternation, he was interrupted with howls of derision early into his delivery and then pelted with water sachets. Edu, who'd stood bemused throughout, called him aside after.

"My chairman, sir, you are not in the university anymore. Our people, the ones who will actually vote, are simple people and most of them did not finish school. I have to show you something, my chairman."

As was conventional, Edu and Osita's growing band of acolytes had taken to addressing him by the title of the position he was contesting for. To do any different would mean that you did not believe Osita was going to win the elections, and that would immediately rank you, in Chief Onwuka's diction, a "betraitor."

Edu dragged Osita off to watch, from a safe distance, a rally by his opponent for the PDP nomination. Uche Emengo, the Great Iroko, was a former thug. He had been a local government councilor several times already. His belly expanded a few more inches during each term he served. He now decided that he was going for the jugular. "Oche Iroko" was his campaign slogan which yielded the double entendre "strong chair" and "Iroko's chairmanship."

Unlike Osita, who had spoken English, the Great Iroko addressed his rally in Igbo. He delved straight into promises of free everything— free primary and secondary education, free water boreholes in every compound, free health centres in every village. Every month, his administration would give a bag of rice and tin of palm oil to every widow in the area. The local government would employ all unemployed youths. No explanation was proffered on how the council's limited finances would cope with even a fraction of these, but the gathering lapped it up.

The Great Iroko spiced his disjointed speech with traditional proverbs, some of them barbs directed at Osita. Midway into the rambling, Iroko's retinue lifted him onto their shoulders and carried him through the audience which spontaneously broke out into song. The popular ditty attested to the villagers' support for Iroko whatever the case:

Iroko, Iroko, Iroko, we'll follow.
If he's going, if he's coming,
Iroko we'll follow.

It was an eye-opening spectacle for Osita. He needed no second telling to adapt his campaign. His Igbo got better with each delivery until he was nearly as fluent as the Great Iroko. He certainly became as glib as his opponent, ditching his statistics in favour of fantastical promises and rabble-rousing.

"A great man once said," Edu told him, in reference to Iroko's manner of speech, "that proverbs are the palm oil by which words are consumed among our people." Osita forced himself to become adept at speaking in parable, a practice he previously derided as "uncivilised." He sat for several nights learning proverbs under his father's tutelage. He reserved a few choice ones for the Great Iroko, mocking his opponent's vulgarity and celebrating Osita's refinement by contrast.

"When a man—like my opponent—does not know where he is going, any road will do. Do we choose someone to send on an errand because he can drink *kai-kai*? No, we choose him because he knows something. We cannot live beside the river and be washing our hands in spit. A vulture is a vulture; no matter how high it flies, it will never become an eagle. Even the biggest Iroko is nothing but chaff when it encounters a determined axe."

Osita was bent on showing off his superior education. Wiser now, he sought to do it in a way that would not alienate his audience. He began to end his speeches with a pithy assertion.

"It was those that spoke Latin, the language of *ukochukwu*—God's missionaries—who said '*Aluta Continua, Victoria Acerta*' which means that our struggle continues but victory is sure. So I greet you all: *Aluta Continua*!"

The villagers quickly picked up on the refrain "*Victoria Acerta*," all the while loving the subtle reminder that while the candidate spoke otherwise in accessible idiom, he possessed a learning and sophistication beyond their fathom. Osita was, therefore, a worthy ambassador—the type of person that Adimora could point outsiders to and proclaim, "we have somebody."

Osita's popularity rose. The marketplaces and motor parks became animated with discussion of the prospects for a *dokinta* chairman. Inebriated patrons of beer parlours acknowledged one another with cries of "Alootah Container." On school playgrounds, children sang the campaign anthem, "Call Him Doctor, He Will Answer," that Edu had cannily composed to the tune of a church hymn.

News filtered that a surprised Great Iroko was getting increasingly agitated. And desperate. It was Edu again who advised Osita to do the needful.

"Chair, you know it is only a tree that will stand still while it is about to be cut down; trust me, your opponent is not a tree despite his name of acclaim."

"What do you mean?" Osita queried.

"My chairman, sir, our land is not the white man's land. Here the spirits of the land are still enormously powerful. Your opponent will be making all sorts of charms now to cripple or even kill you. The deaf need no telling that war has broken out. You have to protect yourself."

Osita was steadfast in his refusal to consult the *dibia* that Edu recommended. Instead, he opted for a Pentecostal preacher. Kachi Diaso had grown up with Osita, but since taking to the ministry had become known only as Prophet Holy Thunder Fireman. Osita had laughed when he first heard what he considered a ludicrous name but found the laugh was on him as his former classmate soon garnered the biggest flock for miles. As his ministry prospered, so had Fireman; his fleet of exotic cars was now surpassed only by those of Cleanout and, of course, Chief Onwuka.

Prophet Fireman embraced Osita in front of the congregation on the appointed Sunday. After Osita had "sown a seed" by making a sizeable cash offering, as commanded by Fireman, the effervescent preacher proceeded to pray for the candidate in typical fire-and-brim-stone style. The prayer ended with an anointing during which Fireman placed his hand on Osita's forehead and spoke in tongues.

Osita was familiar with the procedure: the power of the anointing was supposed to literally fell him. He did not feel the expected spiritual propulsion as Fireman continued unintelligibly, but he obligingly fell backwards anyway. It would not look good if it appeared that any malevolent spirits attending him, perhaps even foisted upon him by his opponent, were so powerful that they prevented him from receiving Fireman's anointing.

Whether it was the efficacy of Fireman's prayers or sheer adrenaline, Osita found that he bore the demands of the campaign rather well. Usually, whenever he kept a series of late nights or did not eat well, he would come down with malaria or, depending on who was diagnosing the feverish symptoms, typhoid. Now, his days did not end before midnight and began before the sun rose. There was always a meeting to attend or someone or group to endear his campaign to. Sometimes he ate too much; sometimes he didn't eat at all. But he kept well, and whatever supernatural forces the Great Iroko might have tried to unleash did not have any visible effect.

As his campaign gathered steam and popular acclaim grew, Osita received donations from far and wide. On the eve of the PDP primaries, he found he was running a surplus. By all accounts, it was still going to be close between him and the Great Iroko. Edu advised him that when elections were tight like that, Chief Onwuka usually swung things the way of the candidate that most impressed him.

Edu was out in the field, supervising last-minute things, when Osita had a brain wave. He would curry Chief Onwuka's favour by proving conclusively that he was going to be an honest chairman. Without telling Edu, he called on Onwuka and tendered one million naira, explaining that it was change from the seed money that Onwuka had given him.

"The big masquerade of Adimora. The leopard that watches over the community. The chief that is greater than his peers. You are praised at home, you are praised abroad and you are praised all over the world. As God has blessed you, so have you dispensed blessings to the poor. Our people say that one spoon of soup in a time of need is more valuable than the whole pot when there is abundance. You fed me a big spoon when I was in famine. I will, however, not be like the man who choked because he took another mouthful before swallowing what was already in his mouth. They say that if you want to know the end, you should look at the beginning. Anyone who can steal an egg will steal the poultry. As God is my witness, Doctor Osita Anumba is incapable of stealing an ant."

Chief Onwuka looked at Osita in disbelief and then burst out laughing before grasping him in a bear hug.

"*Dokinta*, I have not asking you for change? This money is your money. If Chief Onwuka are needing money, it is not this kind of money I am need. Keep it, my son. I know you are try to show honest but keep it. Alootah must container even if Victoria echetram."

Election Day went well. The party delegates from all the wards formed orderly queues and voted from noon at the Amaoye primary school which the party had chosen as voting center. The voting was not only for chairmanship candidates. Delegates also voted for councilors. There were twelve councilor positions, and several candidates had made the cut to contest each nomination. Voting was long, ending after sundown.

The PDP had only a ramshackle office in the local government area. The last time the party tried to use it for vote collation, a disgruntled candidate had thrust the legs of a chair into the rotating ceiling fan. The machine-gun sound that resulted had sent everyone scampering for cover. In the confusion, the candidate grabbed the filled results sheets and started eating them. When order was eventually restored and he was rounded on, all he could say for himself was, "Water, please."

A more secure and spacious place was needed today. The ballots were therefore escorted to Chief Onwuka's residence which was under heavy guard. Only party bigwigs, sundry men of influence and the chairman candidates were admitted into the expansive compound. The various retinues and curious onlookers were kept outside under inadequate canopies erected in the dusty field opposite Onwuka's gates. A raucous atmosphere developed, continuing through the night as refreshment was served and political songs sung.

Everyone knew that this was when the real primaries started. And ended. Some European potentate of antiquity had said that it was not those who cast votes but those who counted them that mattered. But that was because he had not been here before.

Here, it was those who decided what had been counted that mattered. Whatever the ballots said, in the end it would come down to a list agreed upon after intense horse-trading by the local movers and shakers, now sequestered inside the house of the biggest one of them.

The whole process up until now had been a charade—but an inescapable one. The electioneering had to be done even though everyone knew how the results would be decided. Not to go through the mill of campaigning and lobbying would be to have disrespected the people, an abomination fatal to even the best candidate.

Besides, the exercise was one of those things that spread money around and enabled subsistence for many. Money was given and received at every turn. It was "settlement," the only dividend of democracy that was available to most. Edu, astute as ever, knew he had to break it down to a candidate still brimming with idealism.

"My chair, you see the party officials who screen the candidates? We must settle them. Anybody who is somebody in this process, we must settle. We cannot miss out even one person; otherwise, it can be like the one finger that is dipped in palm oil which ended up staining the whole hand. Ward leaders? Settle. Women leaders? Youth leaders? Anybody called 'leader' in the party? Settle. The people who organise rallies? Them too. And of course those who attend the rallies."

"Huh?" Osita interjected. Edu continued without missing a beat.

"Don't look so surprised, my chair—yes, even those that attend rallies except you want to be talking to empty space. As for the delegates who will vote at the primaries, once they are known, ah, their own settlement will be special. You see, they didn't spend all that money settling those who determined they would be delegates just to come and be looking at candidates' faces o. So you must fill their hearts with enough joy, by putting something they can touch in their hands, to make them cast their votes for you."

Most of the settlement money came from the candidates and their supporters. Edu took care of the settling on behalf of Osita, who salved his conscience by convincing himself that the disbursements continually recounted by Edu were merely "campaign costs." Yet all this was just to qualify one to be in the frame for the final list that would be decided tonight and announced as the results of the primaries.

Chief Onwuka's compound had several mansions. He had dedicated one to the day's proceedings. Osita and the Great Iroko were part of it at first, each jostling to get his preferred candidates for councilor put on the list. Both men knew, the Great Iroko from experience and Osita from being tutored by Edu on the dynamics, that it was dangerous to win the seat without having your loyalists dominate the council. A simple impeachment motion at the council's first meeting would abruptly end the chairman's tenure if the councilors were not his men.

Eventually, Osita and the Great Iroko were banished to a plush anteroom so that the negotiations on the chairmanship candidate could begin. The Great Iroko had waited out this process many times before, albeit outside the compound. He promptly stretched out on the sofa and fell asleep.

Osita was nervous but, given his opponent's countenance, was determined not to show it. He feigned disinterest even as his stomach churned. He wished Edu were with him, but his trusted aide had not been deemed high enough in the hierarchy to merit admission. As the hours passed, his edginess waned, giving way to fatigue. Yet, he could not sleep. By 3:00 a.m., he was in envy and awe of the Great Iroko who had stirred only once, to go to the bathroom, before resuming the snoring.

And then suddenly it was over.

The door to the room opened, and Chief Onwuka's bald pate appeared. Osita could not help but notice that he looked remarkably alert for that time of the morning. The Great Iroko woke with a start, as if on cue. Before he could gather himself, Chief Onwuka curtly told him, "Iroko, I want to talking to my chairman. You are wait here for me, are you understanding me? You are not go anywhere. I will coming back, now-now, to talking to you."

Osita did not believe what he was hearing. The Great Iroko's countenance fell, and he seemed to reduce in size. Osita's heart was now pounding. He could hardly breathe.

Chief Onwuka gave him an expansive smile and said, "*Dokinta*, my chair, please come outside with me."

As Osita stepped out of the room and closed the door on a crest-fallen Great Iroko, Chief Onwuka composed himself. It had been a close election, but the *dokinta* had shaded it on the votes cast. Onwuka was astonished at how well the neophyte had done. Onwuka had made a note to assimilate Edu, the organiser, into his personal staff. "This children have really impress me," he had said over and over as the votes were tallied.

There was only one problem—anyone who accounted honestly for money given to him for campaigns would similarly account for local government money. That would not do, and *dokinta* would have to learn. Onwuka had therefore decided to put the Great Iroko on the list as the PDP's chairmanship candidate for the Adimora local government council.

THE GENERAL

It is a melancholy of mine own...in which my often rumination wraps me in a most humorous sadness (As You like It, 4.1.15–18).

General Ibrahim knew his Shakespeare—of that he had no doubt. But he also knew he was well and truly bored—a situation that left him more than a tad perplexed about ambition and fulfilment. He couldn't trust his singing voice, or he would have belted out a few bars of "(I Can't Get No) Satisfaction." A sudden image in his mind's eye of a wiry rock star wagging a finger brought a rueful smile. If only.

He'd craved power his whole career, starting from the first coup. The young lieutenant he was had listened with rapt attention as the major, the flamboyant leader of a grim-faced quartet, spoke to an incredulous nation the morning after a night spent murdering the prime minister and his cabinet. When martial music came on at the end, all Ibrahim could think of was "A Hard Day's Night."

Ibrahim still grimaced at that broadcast. It had gone down in national legend but, if you listened carefully like he had, amounted to little more than a rambling speech peppered with such nuggets of ambiguity as "doubtful loyalty will be penalised by shooting you; so do not try us or we will just shoot you." In contrast, the general thought, smiling grandly, his ascension speech was the epitome of erudition.

Using his proclivity for English literature and British history to great effect, Ibrahim had quoted Milton and Churchill to a bemused populace that applauded the grammar even if most of it went over their heads. He was determined to go down in history as a statesman rather than the crude dictator, so on the way to read the speech, he had changed the title he was assuming to simply "President." God forbid that he ever be ranked with the fat East African, him of the "His Excellency, Field Marshal, Al Hadji, Doctor, VC, DSO, MC, Lord of All the Animals of the Earth and Fishes of the Seas, Conqueror of the British Empire in General and in Africa in Particular, and the Last King of Scotland."

The army had caught a bug from the first one, and coup followed countercoup. Ibrahim quickly learnt to identify the plots likely to succeed and, by aligning with them, propelled himself up the ranks. The irony was not lost on him, therefore, that when national prominence came, it was from his quelling a coup rather than fueling it.

General Ramat was assassinated at the junction near State House. It would never have happened—at least not at a traffic stop—had the reformist leader not insisted on a pruned-down convoy, shorn of outriders, which would obey traffic rules. The mutineers then took control of the national radio station in the Obalende area, from where they broadcast the obligatory "Fellow Countrymen" speech announcing their seizure of power.

"Shell that place to the ground!" thundered loyalist generals, dressed in mufti just in case, from secure hideouts. Ibrahim, by this time a colonel and the commander of the armoured corps, surrounded the station with tanks. But his conscience would not let him do what he'd been ordered.

The compound was full of cowering civilians who had innocently gone to work that day. Ibrahim considered it bad form for an aspiring statesman to become known as the "Butcher of Obalende." Western governments would not like that, and he would need their support when he made his bid for the top job. Commandeering a megaphone and mumbling "Stairway to Heaven" under his breath, he sweet-talked the renegade soldiers into surrendering without a shot being fired.

Several years and two coups later, Ibrahim crested the summit by toppling his erstwhile friend, the stern and Marxist-leaning General Muhammadu, whose harsh crackdowns, termed "War Against Man-pass-Man," had alienated all but the most radical officers. Not only did the British say "yes" and the Americans "yeah" to the "Genius of Obalende," but a surprising "da" also arrived from behind the Iron Curtain. A delighted Ibrahim spent the next three years consolidating his position.

"Money is a good solider," he announced at his first meeting as head of the Supreme Military Council, to rapturous applause. True to his word, he splashed money from the national coffers as never before, much of it on his constituency. Wonderful new barracks were commissioned with fanfare by the toothy-grinned president who quoted Poe and Kipling at the drop of a peaked cap. Military pay was bumped up and all sorts of perks introduced across the ranks, notably including car loans without a payback date for NCOs and above.

If you were a querulous officer—and there were many at first—you were retired, but with a huge gratuity, or posted out as military attaché to an embassy far away, where your inciting voice could no longer be heard at home. And if you were one of the few who insisted on a principled stance, then a summary jail term or, worse, an "accident" awaited—there were limits of course to all that statesmanship business.

It worked. Newly comfortable soldiers stopped planning coups and concentrated on enjoying the spoils, and spoiling, of the Ibrahim government. Fealty to the general had become the surest way to riches beyond fathom, so why risk a date with a firing squad when there were flashy new cars to drive and women to impress?

And thus it was that Ibrahim became bored, especially after "I'm So Lonesome I Could Cry" took on a new resonance.

Everyone who fraternised with him now seemed to do so either for patronage or out of fear. Even the members of the junta, the inner circle who had acquiesced in his taking power, regarded him warily. They would not relax in his presence, and not one dared address him by his nickname of yore, "Grammar-phone," even at his nudging. He was informed of but not invited to weddings and birthday parties, which, truth be told, was understandable because the president's presence turned simple occasions into events of national security.

If there was one person who loved it all, it was his wife.

Fatimah, or "Her Excellency, the First Lady,'" as she was now known, had undergone a transfiguration. The glitterati who had once sniffed at the "barracks wife" now danced *shoki* if she as much as glanced their way while dropping in at one exclusive gala or the other at the Muson Center. Where before, prestigious women's clubs like the Soroptimist would not have given her the time of day, their leaders now queued for audience at State House, invariably ending with the supplication, "We crave your indulgence, Your Excellency, our mommy, to become our grand patroness."

Blessed with a shrewdness to match her husband's, Fatimah set about empowering the hitherto unknown "office of the first lady."

"Village women really suffer in this country," she announced one night as they retired to bed, "but I am going to change that for good." The general kept mum—even a supreme leader knew better than to argue when her tone was set like that.

The next few months would see Ibrahim constantly amused by the antics of his wife and her coterie of bejeweled friends. Arriving by military helicopter or heavily guarded SUVs in village after remote village, they would make exhortations of the womenfolk, the spectacle always ending with chants of "better life for rural women, better life for rural women!"

To Ibrahim's surprise, it worked. Women's co-operatives started springing up everywhere, and middling officials scrambled to add more women to the workforce. Even he started thinking twice before asking Fatimah to make him a cup of Milo and took instead to crooning "I'm a Believer" to her before bed. Within a year, the World Bank was proclaiming the Better Life campaign as the exemplar for ending gender discrimination in the Third World. *Time* magazine put Fatimah, bejeweled of course, on its cover.

Ibrahim had never seen his wife so happy. For that, he was thrilled; beyond that, he was, quite simply, terribly bored.

On this morning, Ibrahim's mood was not being helped by the dour verse flitting in and out of his head, drowning out the lyrics to "We Gotta Get Out of This Place." Then, quite suddenly, he hit upon an idea. He would get back in touch with friends who had long left the military and were not concerned with government. At least, he hoped, he could talk with them freely about old times without their wondering at his motives and becoming guarded. Yes, that would certainly do the trick—he could become one of "the boys" again, even if only for fleeting periods. He called in his closest aide.

"General, sir, Your Excellency," barked Major Sambo Aribisala, snapping to attention in front of the general's desk and saluting him.

"At ease, Sambo," said Ibrahim. "I've told you to stop all this 'Your Excellency' when we're alone."

"Yes, sir, Your Excellency. I'm sorry, Your Excellency."

"Sambo! Look… Anyway, I don't have your time this morning. Do you remember Colonel Gadaka?"

"Yes, sir, Your Excellency, the former commandant of the Defence Academy?"

"Yes, him. You know we used to be the best of friends?"

"Yes, sir, Your Excellency."

"We used to chase women all the time together," Ibrahim laughed. "Of course, that was before I met she-who-must-be-obeyed."

Ibrahim looked up at Sambo conspiratorially but the major remained stock-still, gaze fixed straight ahead as if on the parade ground. Ibrahim hissed and then laughed some more, this time to himself.

"Those were the days, Sambo, I tell you. I lost touch with him years ago, shortly after he retired. I heard he went back to his hometown, somewhere near Potiskum?"

"I don't know, Your Excellency, but I can ask; we can find him easily."

"Okay, get to it at once and do let me know, okay?"

"Yes, sir, Your Excellency," said Sambo. He saluted and turned round sharply to leave.

"One more thing, Sambo. I am just asking about his welfare, okay? I just want to know how he is. Is that clear? None of that nonsense with Malik, okay?"

"Yes, sir, Your Excellency."

Ibrahim had to add that clarification. Sambo was loyal, but sometimes to a fault. Once, Ibrahim had asked, out of courtesy, about the best man at Sambo's wedding. Two weeks later, Sambo had approached him cautiously.

"Your Excellency, sir, please don't be annoyed. I just wanted to know what to do with Major Malik."

Ibrahim was at a loss. "Malik, your friend? Do what with him? What do you mean?"

"Well, after general asked of him, I called military police to arrest him. He has been in detention since, Your Excellency."

Even with all he had seen over the years, Ibrahim was shocked. He hastily ordered Malik's release but refrained from reprimanding Sambo. He knew enough of power to appreciate that every ruler could do with such blind loyalty from his closest aides.

Thinking back now on the incident, the general chuckled. Perhaps he needed a Canute demonstration. Like the English king of legend, he could take a chair out to Bar Beach and show everyone that even he, the commander-in-chief, could not command the sea. Ibrahim chuckled again. British history was no longer taught in schools. Independence had seen to that. Younger people would probably not know what he was talking about.

The general spent the rest of the day attending to the usual throng of courtesy callers, most of whom were praise singers masquerading as important business lobbyists or community leaders. He signed a decree proscribing the pro-democracy group but made a mental note to appoint its garrulous leader into government—that always worked a treat. He read the papers, including his thorn in the flesh, *The Tribune*, which nicknamed him "Evil Genius." He rather liked the name. It added to his mystique.

He laughed at news of police arresting a man who put on a show as a bodiless head, a trick achieved with inventive carpentry and mirrors. People had flocked to the stall, paying a small fee to take photographs and chat with the head. The police announced gravely that the illusionist was a "nefarious individual" whom they would charge with the offence of OBT—obtaining by trick. Ibrahim hoped that the magistrate would have a better sense of humour. He considered having a word with the inspector-general of police but thought better of it. He should let the law take its course, whatever that was.

"Where law ends, tyranny begins," Ibrahim had proclaimed in his maiden speech, quoting another of his British icons, John Locke. A man of his convictions, Ibrahim strove to ensure that whatever he wanted, a law was made for it. Thus, for instance, was "The Very

Important Persons (Exclusion from Traffic Lights Observance) Decree" enacted, to ensure that Ibrahim's motorcade did not have to stop at traffic lights.

Two days later, Sambo returned to brief Ibrahim.

"Your Excellency, sir, it was really something else, *walahi*. There is no road to that village. In fact, we had to dismount and trek for thirty minutes, through heavy bush, before we reached there. Then come and see the village, sir. Just mud huts everywhere."

"And..."

"Your Excellency, sir, *Olorun,*" Sambo said, calling on God.

"Leave *Olorun* first," Ibrahim snapped. "*Yes?*"

"Sorry, Your Excellency, sorry, sir. We found colonel in one small farm in the bush. He was wearing tattered clothes and using a hoe. Your Excellency, he was very dirty; he looked... *jaga-jaga*. Completely."

"Wonderful!" Ibrahim exclaimed. "Wonderful!"

Sambo paused to study the general's countenance to ensure that it was incredulity being expressed rather than approval of Gadaka's condition. Satisfied it was the former, he continued.

"So, we told him that Your Excellency, President and C-in-C, was asking about him, and that you wanted to know how he was doing."

"And what did he say?" Ibrahim asked impatiently.

"He thanked you very much, Your Excellency, sir. He prayed for Your Excellency for a long time."

"Wonderful!"

"He also said..."

"Yes?"

"General, sir, Your Excellency," Sambo looked down.

"Yes?"

"He said he needed ten thousand naira to repair his lorry so that he could take his yams to the market."

"Ten thousand naira?" Ibrahim shouted. "That's less than five hundred dollars."

"Yes, Your Excellency." Sambo's eyes were still fixed to the floor.

"Wonderful! You hear me? Wonderful!" Ibrahim shuddered and fell silent.

Gadaka, the brightest cadet in their set at military college? The Gadaka that was as quick dissembling and reassembling a firearm as solving a complicated mathematical problem? That same Gadaka? Reduced to this?

Perhaps he should not have been surprised. An officers' officer who believed the military had no business in government, Gadaka had retired early, at the rank of colonel, unable to stomach the refusal to return the country to civilian rule. Ibrahim had always questioned such idealism. Ambition, he was convinced, had to be made of sterner stuff.

Sambo's nervous cough brought Ibrahim out of his torpor.

"How big exactly did you say this farm was, Sambo?"

"Very small, Your Excellency, sir—less than one bush plot."

"In other words, a little patch of ground that had no profit in it but the name?"

"I'm sorry, Your Excellency but... I'm sorry, sir, I don't understand."

"It's... No, don't worry, Sambo, it's just something...I learnt in school. Here is what you do. Send someone immediately to Gadaka with one hundred thousand naira. Make sure it reaches him today."

"Yes, sir, Your Excellency."

"And what's the name of that man we made the minister of agriculture the other day?"

"Professor Abdullahi, Your Excellency?"

"Yes, that's him. Get him on the phone for me now."

A month later, Sambo saluted Ibrahim.

"Your Excellency, sir, Colonel Gadaka to see you, Your Excellency."

"Oh fantastic, Sambo. Take him into my private meeting room; I'll see him there."

Ten minutes later, Ibrahim walked into the meeting room. The retired Colonel Mustapha Gadaka immediately threw himself onto the floor, arms outstretched over his head.

"Your Excellency, my brother, my savior. You are now my father. Your Excellency, I won't get up from this floor. I say I won't get up. March on me, step on me, but I won't get up. How can I stand in your presence?"

The General had experienced many outrageous displays of adulation in his time, but he was still embarrassed by this. He was also deeply moved. Bending down and reaching under his friend, Ibrahim gently helped Gadaka up. Gadaka was in tears. Ibrahim guided him to a chair and then sat in studied silence, humming "The Weight" in his head, as the retired colonel struggled for composure.

In between sobs, Gadaka blurted out his gratitude. Ibrahim thought it best to let him finish before saying anything.

"...So Your Excellency, I am too happy. Even after that money you gave me, the minister sent for me and gave me a contract of one million naira. I couldn't believe it. It was to supply—"

"Did you say *one million naira?*" Ibrahim interjected.

"Err...yes, Your Excellency, sir. Erm, I... I..."

Ibrahim's face clouded with rage. He was no longer listening. Motioning for Gadaka to stop, he pressed a button on his desk. Sambo arrived on cue.

"Have the secretary to the government report to my office at once. Then arrange for Colonel Gadaka to spend the night at one of the federal government guest houses—make sure it is one of the best, one of those we reserve for visiting heads of state."

"Yes, sir, Your Excellency."

Ibrahim made his excuses to Gadaka, saying he had remembered an urgent matter of state that needed his attention. Ibrahim managed his trademark toothy grin and gave Gadaka a bear hug to reassure the visibly frightened former soldier that he was neither the cause nor object of the president's sudden agitation.

That night, it was announced on national television that Professor Abdullahi had been removed as the minister of agriculture "with immediate effect" and placed under arrest for embezzling a large sum belonging to the ministry. Mustapha Gadaka, "a distinguished retired colonel and lately a successful agriculturalist" would take over, again with immediate effect, at the ministry.

Sambo watched the news in the general's darkened office with him.

When it was over, Ibrahim spoke. "That idiot of a professor, he will go to prison for a long time. I will make sure of that. The president instructs you to give someone a contract and it is only a one-million-naira contract you give? Can you imagine? He's a foolish man, bloody civilian like him. Canute can wait."

"Yes, sir, Your Excellency."

"Do you know Canute, Sambo?"

"No, sir, Your Excellency. Should we arrest him?"

THE OFFERING

Uduak shifted uneasily in his seat. He felt his undershirt start to soak. He had broken out in cold sweat. If this continued for a little longer, he would soak through to his new shirt. He had bought the shirt for the special occasion today. It was a "superior" shirt, a Hackett in sky blue that he'd craved for a long time. The last thing he wanted was for it to be soiled on its first outing. But even that was a small matter compared to the decision he now faced.

The voice of Mfon Okon, known to the faithful gathered here as simply "Pastor," rang out again.

"And I say argh, the Lord argh, has revealed to me argh, that today argh, today argh, someone argh, someone here will make an offering argh, an offering of his car to the Lord argh. Praise the Lord argh!"

The congregation responded. "Alleluia."

Pastor was not satisfied. "That Alleluia is strangled. That Alleluia sounds paralyzed. I say praise the lord aargh!"

The response went up several decibels. "Alleluia!!!"

Uduak joined the louder chorus but his voice was weak. He patted the pocket where his keys were.

Pastor's voice filled the small church again. "The Lord argh, is testing argh! Our almighty Lord argh, the alpha and omega, is testing argh!"

The pastor's inflection made the "testing" come out as "tasting." Uduak wondered ruefully whether that was also a sign from the Lord. He could well taste the fear at where this was heading.

"Praise the Lord argh!"

"Alleluia!!!"

Uduak put his hand into his pocket and closed it around the car keys. The keys to the car that had become his property less than five days ago. The used, "Tokunbo" car he had slaved and saved for. The car that had taken him three years of countless prayers and offerings, not to talk of a small miracle, to afford. Surely, the Lord who so graciously provided it could not be demanding that he, Uduak, give up this car, the car he called his "covenant car," immediately?

"Let us go to Genesis, chapter twenty-two."

Pastor paused, mopping his brow as pages of bibles swished, seeking the passage he directed. He was resplendent in a white suit, even though, as Uduak knew, the suit was bought in the same "bend-down," used-clothes market that most of the congregation, including Uduak, patronised. The shirt under Pastor's suit, white also, had been pristine at the start of the service but was now saturated with perspiration.

The sweaty parallels brought scant consolation to Uduak. Pastor was soaked because he was exerting himself under the klieg lights of the altar. Uduak's sweat was borne not of similar labours but of sheer panic.

"Are you there? Praise the Lord?"

"Alleluia!"

"Read verse one and verse two," Pastor said, turning to the assistant pastor at the lectern.

The assistant obliged as Pastor sat down on his throne, a big wooden chair in the center of the altar, placing his wireless microphone on his lap. "Now it came to pass after these things that God tested Abraham and said to him, 'Abraham!' And he said, 'Here I am.' Then He said, 'Take now your son, your only son Isaac, whom you love, and go to the land of Moriah, and offer him there as a burnt offering on one of the mountains of which I shall tell you.'"

Pastor sprang up. "Did all of us hear that? God tested Abraham. Abraham, the father of Israel. The father of God's chosen people. God did what? God tested him."

The last three words were said slowly as if there was a full stop after each. Uduak felt his stomach churn the way it ordinarily only did when he ate too much beans. Who was he, Uduak, compared to Abraham? Who was he not to do the Lord's bidding by submitting to this clear and present "taste"?

"So what did Abraham do? Verse three."

The reader obliged once more. "So Abraham rose early in the morning and saddled his donkey and took two of his young men with him, and Isaac his son; and he split the wood for the burnt offering, and arose and went to the place of which God had told him."

Pastor still stood in the front of the altar, microphone gripped close to his chest with both hands. As the reading of the verse ended, he freed his right hand, moving it in an arc that went upwards first then sharply down until his arm was outstretched and his palm open, pointing downwards.

"You see? Can you see? Abraham obeyed the Lord his God, the Lord our God! No asking about. No thinking about. Oh my God. Praise the Lord?"

"Alleluia."

Uduak closed his fist over the keys. If he could have burrowed them deeper into his trousers, he would have. He tried to distract himself by reflecting on Pastor's habit of leaving out "it" after saying "about." It was amusing ordinarily, but not today.

"Now go to verses nine and ten."

The assistant took over again. "Then they came to the place of which God had told him. And Abraham built an altar there and placed the wood in order; and he bound Isaac his son and laid him on the altar; upon the wood. And Abraham stretched out his hand and took the knife to slay his son."

Pastor went into a frenzy. He jumped up and down on the stage and then started running in place. His head was bent into his chest. His elbows were squeezed tight to his sides, the microphone gripped two-fisted and held close to his mouth. His eyes were screwed shut.

"Oh my God! You hear that? Did you hear that? Oh my God! Oh my God!"

The congregation responded to Pastor. Some mimicked his frenetic knees-up jig. Others shook their hands vigorously above their heads, eyes shut. Some knelt and some stood—Uduak among the latter. Several at the ends of rows stepped out from the wooden benches into the aisles.

"My people, my people, you hear that? God told him to sacrifice his only son. Can you imagine? Abraham did not ask question of God. No, no, no. He heard God's call and he obeyed!!! Oh my God. Oh my God!!!"

Uduak felt himself welling up. The tears began to run, mixing with the sweat on his face. He wanted to believe he was blubbing at the rhapsody that Pastor was invoking among the congregated. A guilt-laden inner voice warned him, *My friend, do not deceive yourself there; it is that car that is making you cry o.*

"He is asking you, *yew, and yew, yew* to bring your car key and make it an eternal offering to the Lord. Surrender! Surrender! Surrender your car to the service of the Lord!"

Uduak wondered, through his tears, why the Lord was demanding the car from him. Why didn't the Lord just give another car, a brand new one, to the church? His answer came immediately.

"Are you questioning, God, brother? Are you? Are you more than Abraham? God spoke to Abraham one-to-one, but he did not question. So who are you? I say who are you? Who are to question?"

Taken aback by Pastor's seeming telepathy, Uduak looked desperately to Susan in the choir by the side of the altar. His beloved fiancée had danced for joy when he drove straight to hers after he took delivery of the car. Her mother, coming out to see what the commotion was, wept when she realised that her daughter would be marrying a car owner—that was more than she had achieved with Papa Susannah of blessed memory.

"Yield argh! The Lord is saying to you to yield! Am I talking to somebody? Somebody argh. Yield argh. Follow the example of Abraham! Wherever you are, if you are in the front, if you in the back, if you are on the side, yield argh! Yield argh!"

Uduak caught Susan's eyes when she looked up briefly. The moment passed too quickly for him to make out a message. No sooner had she raised her head than she turned her attention again to the Bible that was open in her hands. She was mouthing a prayer furiously, her head bobbing like the prayer warrior she was. He knew Susan. She would be begging the Lord to open his heart.

"Yield to the test. Do not listen to the tempter. For what shall it profit a man to gain the world and lose his soul?"

It was Susan that had first brought him to this church. He believed in the Scriptures but that was about it. He did not see any need to go to church every Sunday or, like Susan did, every evening, to convince God that he was worthy of salvation.

Susan insisted. This was a powerful new man of God, she said, with an indisputable anointing. The members of his flock recounted miracles that were wrought by his prayers weekly. Perhaps, even Uduak's long-standing efforts at buying a car could be rewarded if they both prayed together as part of Pastor's flock.

Eventually, Uduak had relented. "Only on Sundays though," he warned. She conceded in turn but with a wry smile that seemed to say, *Okay, for now; I am woman and in time, we'll get exactly where I want.*

Pastor had started the church as a daily prayer meeting in his room and parlour in Ajegunle barely a year ago. Up to his heeding the calling, Pastor had been just another "area father" scrounging a ghetto living and smoking weed in his spare time. He drove a beat-up *keke* with which he ferried people, for a fee, in and out of the nooks and crannies of "Jungle City." Now, he had found favour in the eyes of the Lord, and his ministry was "moving," as the faithful would say.

Indeed, Pastor's ministry was moving so much that services had been relocated to a small hall at the end of Pastor's street. Standing lights and a sound system were rented for Sunday service from DJ Pasuma on the same street. Pastor made a show of blessing the equipment before each service to exorcise any unclean manifestations, such as the spirit of fornication or that of drunkenness, which their worldly use the night before might have attracted.

Uduak tried to get a grip on himself. He was relieved that he was in church. People did not laugh here at a grown man crying. Rather, they respected you for it. You were in raptures, possessed by the spirit. Crying was a sign of your piety and surrender to the Almighty.

"The Lord is calling for you to provide a car sacrifice. You have suffered. You have suffered. And you have a car you love so much. But God is calling you today. He is calling you as he called Abraham. Abraham waited and suffered before he had a son. Where are you? Can you hear Him? It is you the Lord is calling. Where is our Abraham of today? Where are you, the Lord's faithful servant?"

Uduak wanted to say "Here I am" but, instead, he unclenched his fist slowly and carefully removed it from his side pocket. Even with the din going on in the church, he was afraid that if the keys jangled in his pocket, the worshippers next to him might realise that it was him resisting the divine call. He did not know of anyone else in the congregation who had a car. Even Pastor still came and went on his *keke*.

Deliberately, trying not to move his right leg, Uduak put his hand in his back pocket and brought out his handkerchief. After wiping his eyes and his face, he put the handkerchief into his side pocket, pushing it down onto the keys as a buffer against any sound.

Pastor called out again. "Where is our Abraham aargh? Where is the man argh that the Lord argh has called argh? He is not answering? Okay, please read verse eleven."

The assistant obliged again. "But the Angel of the Lord called to him from heaven and said, 'Abraham, Abraham!' So he said, 'Here I am.'"

Uduak was astounded. Everything seemed to be indicating a call to him from the Most High. The very words he, Uduak, had felt compelled to utter moments ago were the ones Abraham had used to answer. It was surely the same angel that had called Abraham that was now calling him through Pastor.

"*El Shaddai, Adonai.* We shall lift up your name; we shall bless you with our car offering."

Uduak felt his fate—and that of the car—being sealed. Still, he could not bring himself to go up to the altar. He looked again at Susan, hoping for any kind of sign from her that he could cling to in exculpation. His wife-to-be was evidently caught in the fervor of the moment. She was no longer reading the Bible. Her face was turned towards the ceiling, her eyes shut. She was swaying from side to side, hands held high and lips moving furiously.

Uduak glanced around him. Much of the congregation was doing the same as his Susan. The craziness had mostly been reigned in since

Pastor had stopped running in place. It was now feverish enunciation rather than rabid motion. Pastor was like a conductor with the congregation. He signaled and they followed. Currently, he had one hand up in the air with the other holding the microphone close to his mouth.

"*Ohashana gbantashan shangolago namashegay asharara klaatu barada nikto!*"

Pastor had begun praying in tongues, the highest form of beseeching in the spirit. Uduak knew he had to join. He put his hand in his pocket and closed his fist over handkerchief and keys. He brought out the hand, keys covered by the handkerchief, and raised his fist over his head. He furiously mouthed words that he did not understand, trying to block out the voice in his head that kept urging him to go forwards to the altar.

"*Shandilyaimai shundai himmalalpa shantisinki kumi shinti alapa-lalama shokolokobangoshay!*"

Something told him to look again at his fiancée. Lo and behold, Susan was staring across at him with a smile like that she had given when he'd accepted to start going to church with her. It was a knowing grin that made Uduak feel she was laughing secretly at him. Then she nodded, nearly imperceptibly at first but gradually in a more pronounced way.

Uduak smiled back sheepishly in resignation. He considered her message clear. To some degree, if only a minuscule one, he was consoled. If his fiancée had accepted prayerfully that they go back to walking long distances and catching rickety, overcrowded Lagos *danfo* buses, then so be it.

"Our Lord is good?" Pastor was ending the speaking in tongues.

"All the time!"

"Amen?"

"Amen!"

Pastor mopped his brow repeatedly. He was beaming at the congregation, his eyes searching. Uduak noticed that even the underarm of Pastor's jacket had developed a damp patch. Uduak looked at his own shirt. It was soaked through, but he no longer cared. The sadness he now felt was from the imminent loss of another possession that was much more prized.

There was relative calm and little but a low hum in the church as congregants and Pastor collected themselves from their linguistic exertions. Uduak lowered his hands and made to extricate the keys from his handkerchief so he could wipe his face before proceeding to the altar. His hands were sweaty and shaking.

To Uduak's chagrin, the keys slipped and fell under the wooden bench in front of him. The sound they made when they hit the cement floor might as well have been gunfire to his ears. He was sure the whole church heard it. For confirmation, he looked at the worshipper to his right. The man smiled at him, shrugging. Uduak grimaced. There was no way out now—if ever there was a sign that he had to give up the car, this was it.

As Uduak bent down to pick up the keys, he heard Pastor make a request again of the reader. "Verse fifteen to seventeen."

Uduak straightened up. The keys, back in his hand, felt like hot coals.

"Then the Angel of the Lord called to Abraham a second time out of heaven. And said: 'By Myself I have sworn, says the Lord, because you have done this thing, and have not withheld your son, your only son. Blessing I will bless you and multiplying I will multiply your descendants as the stars of the heaven and as the sand which is on the seashore; and your descendants shall possess the gate of their enemies.'"

"Did you hear that, brethren?" Pastor's voice was low.

Uduak looked at his keys one last time.

"Did you hear that? Sow the seed of faith and our Father will multiply you. Come forward now so that you can start to multiply. Do not block your destiny. This, your one small car today, will become a convoy of big jeeps tomorrow. You shall see car and see car and see car till you say, 'No, Lord, forget about; I don't want again.' Come now, brother."

Uduak started to make his way out of the bench, his eyes set on the ground to avoid stepping on congregants' legs.

On cue, Pastor's voice went up an octave. "I see you, brother, I see you! Come on! Come and sow the seed of car! Sow it in joy argh! Sow it in faith argh. Your harvest shall never ever cease!"

Uduak had not yet reached the aisle but inclined his head sideways to acknowledge Pastor.

Pastor was shouting excitedly now. "Come argh, come argh, brother! Come and *giiiiive* to the Lord argh. Luke six, thirty-eight argh. Give and it shall be given unto you. Come forth argh! Come argh, come argh, come argh! Hosanna argh argh argh!"

Uduak was about to hold up his keys to signal total surrender to divine command when he realised that Pastor was not looking in his direction. He followed Pastor's gaze and saw Akpan the meat seller, about five rows ahead of him on the other side of the aisle, holding a set of keys up above his head and dancing out with his wife.

Pastor broke into song. "For he is a miracle-working God, he is a miracle-working God…"

The choir and congregation enthusiastically took up the refrain. "He's the alpha and omega, he's a miracle-working God."

Uduak had reached the aisle by this time, but so had other worshippers, some whipping out their phones to take photographs of Akpan and his wife offering their car keys to Pastor. Uduak stopped in his tracks. He didn't know whether to laugh or cry at first but shortly broke into a delirious cackle.

"He's a miracle-working God…"

Uduak pocketed his keys and danced back to his seat. His singing rang as loud as anyone else's. "He's a miracle-working God…"

Uduak was so happy and relieved that he thought his heart would burst out of his chest. He had never enjoyed service as he did the rest of the day's proceedings. It was only at the end that it began to dawn on him that he would have some explaining to do with Susan. He prepared himself.

As a rule, the choir members tarried after service for debriefing by the choirmaster. Uduak waited patiently in the car for Susan to join him. He was elated at still being able to pick her up in a car. When eventually she climbed into the passenger's seat, she embraced him warmly. Then she reared back to regard him.

"What's the matter, dear?" she asked, noticing the furrowed brow.

"I hope you're not disappointed, honey?" Uduak responded sheepishly.

"Disappointed? Why?"

"Well, I saw you praying, praying and praying. Then you looked at me and smiled one kind of smile like that. I know you wanted me to make that car offering, eh?"

"Aha. If you knew that, then why didn't you make it, dear?"

Uduak had his hands on the steering wheel, looking straight ahead. But he could see Susan out of the corner of his eye. He had expected reproach but was finding it neither in her voice nor in the smile that seemed to be playing on her lips.

"I'm sorry, baby. I just couldn't… I mean I was about to go but then…then, Akpan and his wife…they went. When did he even buy a car? I didn't know he bought a car."

He turned to look at Susan. There was still merely that hint of a smile, but what was it then that made him feel he was being laughed at?

"I'm so sorry baby," he continued. "I know I disappointed you. I know I betrayed your revelation in the Spirit. Now because of me, because I couldn't sacrifice something of this world like a car, we will miss our multiplication of blessings."

"Maybe not, darling," said Susan, touching his hand gently.

"What do you mean?"

"Bring out your Bible, baby."

Ordinarily, Uduak would have argued at another Bible lesson from Susan so soon after church, but today he was drained. He reached wordlessly to the back seat and retrieved his Bible.

"You remember Pastor was referring us to Genesis twenty-two during the offertory?" Susan asked.

"Erm, yes, but I thought…"

"What did you *thought*, dear?" She was clearly mocking him now, albeit sweetly.

"What do you mean?"

"What do I mean? Well, read verses twelve to fourteen. Pastor did not ask us to read those ones."

Uduak opened to Genesis twenty-two and found the relevant verses. He read them under his breath. "And the Angel of the Lord said, 'Do not lay your hand on the lad, or do anything to him; for now I know that you fear God, since you have not withheld your son, your only son, from Me.' Then Abraham lifted his eyes and looked, and there behind him was a ram caught in a thicket by its horns. So Abraham went and took the ram and offered it up for a burnt offering instead of his son. And Abraham called the name of the place, The-Lord-Will-Provide as it is said to this day, 'In the Mount of the Lord it shall be provided.'"

He was grinning as he finished, but he was still confused. "So dear, it... I don't understand... You were nodding...?" he queried.

"Yes, dear, I was trying to tell you, 'Don't worry, everything is going to be okay.' I didn't want you to do anything foolish. I know you. So I prayed and prayed for our own sacrificial lamb. I knew my prayers would be answered."

For the second time that afternoon, Uduak broke into a delirious laugh.

A POT OF SOUP

Buchi wanted home-cooked Nigerian food. He would do anything for *fufu* and vegetable soup right now. He was tired of all the restaurant chains that Shaniqua loved to dine at. She was particularly fond of the Pappadeaux Seafood on Westheimer Road, near the Galleria. She always started with the shrimp and crawfish fondue served with garlic bread. Her favored entrée was the Mississippi catfish opelousas. The cocktail of choice, constantly replenished and doubling as dessert, was an apple martini.

Shaniqua, Shaniqua. Buchi's beloved African American girlfriend. She never cooked so that even when they did not dine out, they ordered via Uber Eats. On Sundays, depending on when they woke up, they would go to the Breakfast Klub in midtown or Mamma's Oven on the south side. Both served variations of soul food. Buchi liked soul food, particularly the oxtail. He considered it the nearest that American cuisine had to African food.

All this was a bit heavy on the wallet, and Buchi wished for different sometimes, especially as he was up to the task if the menu comprised Nigerian food. He considered himself quite the gourmet chef when it came to okra, *egusi* or *onugbu* soup. Friends who ate his *jollof* rice—cooked the original way rather than the Ghanaian imitation—readily confirmed that it had no "part two." Whenever he made pepper soup, it was "off the chain," as Shaniqua would have said if she appreciated the finer points of Nigerian gastronomy.

As much as he loved the food and was adept at preparing it, Buchi rarely cooked. First was the inconvenience. The ingredients for Nigerian cooking were not available at Walmart or Kroger. One had to go all the way to southwest Houston, where Africans and especially Nigerians congregated, to find the right shops. But even that was a trifling compared to Buchi's main reason for avoidance—he did not want to invite the less savory side of Nigerian food into his home.

Buchi would be the first to acknowledge that the object of his desire did give off a strong smell. Where aficionados would perceive an appetizing aroma and respond with stirred palates, the uninitiated might be discomfited by an overpowering of their olfactory senses. If you cooked a pot of Nigerian soup or stew, the smells seeped into the walls and hung heavy in the air for days so that air fresheners, made with less formidable tasks in mind, were of little relief.

When he was small, Buchi thought that traditional homes in Nigerian villages had their kitchens as outhouses to protect the main houses from the dangers of open fires. It was only when he came to America that he realized the deeper wisdom of his ancestors.

Many of the Nigerian homes he knew in Houston smelled permanently of the food, open-plan living spaces with shuttered windows proving a potent incubator for the vigorous aromas. The inhabitants rarely noticed, although they would comment heartily on the smell of garlic whenever they visited the residence of an Indian friend.

Today, however, Buchi yearned for Nigerian food. He could have driven to any of the restaurants in Little Nigeria, the stretch of Bissonnet west of I-59, but he liked neither their ambiance nor their customer service, or rather lack of it. The deed would therefore have to be done at home.

Shaniqua was not expected back until Tuesday. Since the cooking and imbibing were going to be a one-off, he would have three days to get rid of any telltale smells so that his girlfriend would be none the wiser.

Shaniqua worked for Southwest Airlines. The first time he'd addressed her as an "air hostess," she flew into a rage. It was "flight attendant," she yelled at him, "like a brain surgeon, a *professional!*" The term he'd used was "wack and retarded," putting her on par with "ratchet hoochies up in them clubs with scraggly-ass weaves" who did nothing other than welcome patrons with a smile and make sure they were suitably seated.

The offensive description would be permanently excised from his vocabulary when Shaniqua nearly screeched his head off at a subsequent slip of tongue. Buchi smiled. His girl was drama. Little things set her off. His friends who met her said she was the reason they would never mess with "*akata*"—African American—women, talk less of dating them; their *wahala* was too much.

Buchi smiled some more. If *akata* women were feisty, it was in a way he found all too appealing. Shaniqua's combustibility was a far cry from the submissiveness of African women his age, which he saw through from miles away and loathed. He rarely passed up an opportunity to call the marriage-material act a "put-a-ring-on-it 419."

Still, he would have liked Shaniqua to have had a fraction—just a teeny-weeny, little, small fraction—of the willingness of many a woman of any culture to cook and clean for her man. Buchi picked up around the house after Shaniqua. He would vacuum while she watched yet another episode of *Love & Hip Hop*, double apple martini in hand. She hated doing the dishes, even if that meant simply plonking them in the dishwasher.

Buchi also took care of the laundry. He smiled at the thought of what his friends and even his mother would say if they saw him sorting out her underwear for the wash. "What? *Chineke* God, that *akata* woman has turned you into a woman wrapper!" It was anathema, the height of loss of manliness, for an African like him to wash a woman's panties, even if that woman was his significant other.

Shaniqua was a handful, but he was crazy about her. Not only was she stunning, but her dress sense rendered "provocative" an understatement. Her friends called her "Black Barbie," a nickname Buchi pooh-poohed as not doing his bootylicious girl justice. He would always say that her body must have been made on a Monday when the Almighty was at his creative best after having rested on Sunday.

Buchi could not keep his eyes or hands off Shaniqua. Everything about her gave him a rise—the thought of which immediately brought stirrings to his loins. But he quelled himself—he was not unfaithful and would, "by fire by force" as Nigerian preachers loved to say, keep any longings at bay until she came back.

Buchi liked that Shaniqua had no issues with her complexion. She was dark and proud, did not use toning creams, and thought crazy the African women who did. "What's wrong with y'all?" she would ask Buchi, laughing at before-and-after pictures of yet another Nigerian woman who'd had skin-whitening treatments. Buchi always stifled the urge to say, "Wait till you see some Congolese men."

Shaniqua had also begun to lean toward her natural hair, wearing afros and foreswearing straighteners. Gone were all the Malaysian and Brazilian "100-percent human" hair extensions, and in their place the washing, blow dry, and styling at Afro Sisi, the salon on Pearland's Broadway that did only natural hair. She emerged looking even more glamorous in Buchi's eyes and those of other men, who stopped in their tracks when the nappy-haired goddess strode by.

Shaniqua had never tried African food, and Buchi was not about to broach the subject. Before her, he had briefly dated another *akata*, Marquesha, whom he'd taken to the Cameroonian restaurant on West Belfort to sample the signature grilled croaker and plantains. She'd found it all too peppery and had been repulsed by the sight of the head, the fish having been served whole as was customary. Marquesha was not nearly as bougie as his current girlfriend so he had never bothered to raise a similar experience with Shaniqua.

Today, Buchi yearned for his Nigerian soup filled with *orishirishi* accompanied by pounded yam or some other *fufu*. It would be in keeping with his fashion of reconnecting with his roots, however briefly, whenever Shaniqua was away. The night before, he had made sure to go to inDmix at Belvedere. The afrobeat was as much off the chain to him as was, to Shaniqua, the trap music that they danced to in clubs of her choice downtown.

Yes o, it was the turn of *Naija* food to go down today. Buchi laughed as he grabbed his keys. His countrymen loved their nicknames; you couldn't take that away from them. No less than an information minister had found as much when her efforts to ban the use of "*Naija*," for "belittling the giant of Africa," proved to be as successful as fetching water in a basket.

He drove down I-59, salivating at the prospect of the dish he was about to make. He missed Shaniqua, but the opportunity to indulge his palate in her absence provided some comfort. Thinking about her made him wonder for the umpteenth time at her name. He had heard somewhere that *akata* imagined names like hers to sound African, starting from the radical 1960s. He wondered why, if that were true, they had not simply asked the Africans all over America for authentic names.

When a famous African American actor took potshots at names like Shaniqua and Marquesha, Buchi was even more perplexed. He did not quite understand why names of such melodic quality should be blamed for problems in the hood. He'd raised it once with Shaniqua, jokingly, and she'd hit the roof. Not only did Buchi not dare mention the matter again, but the actor's star had since waned after his being outed as a serial molester.

Buchi liked the ring of Danisha, Dejuante and, of course, Shaniqua. He had long grown bored of the likes of Jane, Angela, and Mary and, if truth be told, Amaka, Ifeoma, and Titilayo.

He was soon on Bissonnet. It was a few minutes after 2:00 p.m. As usual, there were girls walking down the road in little more than underwear. Buchi had seen streetwalkers in Lagos, particularly on Victoria Island, but only at night. He always wondered if the daytime walkers here included Nigerians but had never stirred up the courage to ask them. If anybody he knew saw him accost one of the girls, there was no telling where the story would get to. The Nigerian community was, after all, large and small at the same time.

As he slowed down to turn into the strip mall that housed the African grocers, one of the girls caught his eye and winked. He reflexively winked back and laughed his way into the parking lot.

Buchi had learned, in his words, to "sanitize Nigerian cooking" so that it was less pungent by substituting some of the traditional condiments. When he cooked the white *nsala,* for instance, he used cream of mushroom soup, from a can, as a thickener instead of cocoyam. Today, however, he was determined to go fully native.

It did not take long to round up the ingredients. He considered dried fish for extra flavor but did not like the look of the ones in the store. He smiled to himself. Back home, dried fish would contain *nna*, the grubs of small insects that fed on the fish when laid out in the sun to dry.

If you recoiled at the sight, older people would laugh and assure you that *nna* in the fish was part of the fish. Certainly, however, if any fish here featured as much as one *nna*, Harris County officials, already suspicious of these exotic "world" foods, would close the grocer for good. Buchi laughed. These Americans didn't know what they were missing.

When it got to his turn at the till, the cashier with tribal marks smiled sheepishly and said, "I'm sorry, sir but the card reader has developed fault." Anywhere else in America, Buchi might have complained in righteous indignation. Here, it was amusing, welcome even. He was back in the motherland in this shop, so he had to be patient with things sometimes not working as he had become used to. "Technician is coming, sir," the cashier offered in encouragement. There was, of course, no technician in sight. Luckily, Buchi had cash.

As he waited to maneuver onto Bissonnet Street, the girl who had winked at him on his way in crossed the road in front of his car, flashing a smile as she trotted by. He grinned back at her, this time voluntarily. The girls had to keep walking lest they be stopped by the police for soliciting. It was only when a potential patron actively signaled intent that the girls went to meet him. Buchi knew the score, having seen it before in the area. His winking girl looked back for further encouragement, but he did not humor her.

It took longer than he expected to get home. There was an accident on the Chimney Rock exit, northbound on the freeway. He always wondered at that exit. An entrance ramp came into the freeway just before the exit. Traffic therefore merged dangerously close to the exit, cars often having to crisscross each other at considerable speed. One evening, after they'd narrowly avoided a collision there, his friend, Ejike, summed it up: "You know, *nwokem*, these Americans are not perfect as people back home think o."

By the time Buchi drove into the condo complex he lived in, his car was suffused with smells that took him back to his childhood.

Crayfish was one of the big culprits but did not hold a candle to *ogili isi*—the *ogili* that smells—that paste of fermented oil seeds used as flavoring for soups. Ejike had been on the money when he remarked once, "Guy, if a people used to strong-smelling food have included 'smell' in the name of one of them, please respect that one o!" Buchi laughed as he took the shopping bags out of the trunk.

He did not waste time getting to work in his kitchen. He washed and wrung the *onugbu*. He tasted a little to make sure the residual bitterness was just right. Satisfied, he set them aside. He washed the cocoyam and cooked it to softness before peeling and grinding it into a smooth paste. He then turned his attention to the *orishirishi,* which he washed thoroughly.

He boiled the *shaki* and *kpomo* first. Then he added the beef, goat meat, and a generous helping of salt. After cooking for about five minutes, he added pepper, crayfish and *ogili*. He waited ten more minutes to add small chunks of the coconut paste and three cooking spoons of palm oil. Everything, save for the bitter leaf, was in.

Buchi licked his lips and turned his attention to the NFL game on TV while his *onugbu* soup came together, bubbling away on high heat. The Houston Texans usually fell short, but he had learned to love them anyway. Houston also had an MLS team, but he preferred to watch the English Premier League, which to him was the epitome of football—he could never get used to calling it "soccer." When Buchi first came to America, he had to drive all the way to a pub on Richmond to have a hope of watching English teams on rare and expensive satellite transmission. Now, all the major networks showed European football. "World champions" had since taken on a different meaning in American sport.

When the cocoyam was completely dissolved, Buchi added the bitter leaf. After cooking for a few more minutes, he dipped the cooking spoon into the pot and let some of the broth drop onto his palm. Tasting the soup off his palm, he decided he had achieved perfection again. He turned down the heat, rubbing his hands in glee. Now, it was on to making the *fufu*. To his horror, he realized he had forgotten to buy any. He slapped his palm against his forehead in frustration. He would have to go out again.

He did the drive to Bissonnet in record time and duly got his *fufu* powder. He was tempted to buy yams instead and do the pounding, but he had neither mortar nor pestle, and the powder took relatively little time to make. Rushing to get back, he forgot that the freeway was snarled at Chimney Rock. It took him over an hour to get home. He bounded up the stairs to his apartment only to sense immediately that something was wrong.

He looked at the stove and there was no pot. He wondered momentarily whether he had put the pot in the fridge before he left. Of course, he could not have—even novices knew to let soup cool down first. Still, he checked the fridge. The pot was not there. He opened the kitchen cabinets, growing more frantic by the minute. There was still no pot of soup.

Buchi looked around, his eyes darting to the windows. The windows were wide open. He was sure they'd been closed when he left. Could someone have broken in and stolen his pot of soup? Such things were known to happen in poorer neighborhoods in Nigeria but surely not here, in affluent America, where everyone was middle class.

Who would want a pot of Nigerian soup anyway? As far as he knew, none of the neighbors were African. He had purposely chosen to live in this complex because there were no other Nigerians here. Just then he heard a noise in the bedroom. It sounded like the shower. He burst into the bathroom. There in her full, naked glory was Shaniqua.

"Hallooooos, pikachuuu," she exclaimed, smothering him in kisses and drenching him.

"Hello, baby," he said tentatively. "But…"

"But what, honey dumpling?" she said, crossing her hands behind his neck. "My boo not happy to see me?"

"Of-of course but you were…"

"Yup, I wasn't supposed to finish today, but some other girl wanted extra work and we agreed to switch in Charlotte. I caught the next flight outta there. So here I am, baby. Are you ready to get turned up tonight or what?"

"Sure, baby," Buchi said. For once, he was distracted despite the dripping Black Barbie whose arms were around him.

"What's the matter, baby?" Her big, round eyes looked up at him inquiringly with the twinkle that he found so alluring.

"No, nothing…"

"Oh, by the way, baby, I leave for two days and y'all gon let some soul food go bad in the house? What's up with that?"

"What do you mean?" Buchi asked, his pulse quickening.

"Well, when I came in, I tell you, something godawful going on, on top of that stove. I opened the pot, and something definitely gone bad in there, mmm, mmm, mmm. Didn't look like nothing I'd ever seen before. And the smell? O-M-G!"

"Wha-what did you do with the pot?"

"Took it downstairs and threw it in the trash. Sure wasn't having none of that in our home, baby. Oh, baby! Let's order us some food."

MARTYR

Amina

It is Friday afternoon. The faithful will soon start gathering for prayers in the house of worship. This *gidan bauta* they are coming to is big. And very beautiful. I adore everything about it—the minarets from where the call to prayer will ring out, the arches on its walls, the painted glass in the arches, everything. And then, eh, just look at the roof: a huge, golden dome. The sun is shining on it. Even from this far away, the whole thing is dazzling my eyes. I won't lie; he chose really well. It is the perfect place to die.

I am sitting under the mango trees at the edge of the square. This is where he told me to be, by the market they are now setting up. Traders need no telling that *Jummah* congregations assure them good custom. They will try to sell everything from prayer beads and mats to *gara* cooking pots to food and drink.

Of course, they also have *kayan mata,* the things for women. *Damagadas* will make your breasts stand up again but *zaman mata,* the honey of women, will make a man always come back to you whether your breasts are reaching for the ground or pointing forwards like arrows. And then, if you try *tsumi,* you will want to do and do. I find myself laughing when I think of this. I can't believe I can still laugh, but I do, to myself.

I see him shortly, making his way through the stalls, dressed in black as usual. Even his turban is black. He is bringing another girl, leading her gently by the hand. Anyone who sees them will think it is a loving baba with his daughter. If only they knew, fa. But they don't. I do.

He motions the girl to sit down, and she does, very gingerly, beside me. He stoops and whispers to her. He points at me but in a very discreet way—if you were not watching carefully, you would not notice. He says nothing to me and departs without a backwards glance.

The new girl and I are a few steps removed from a group of women sitting similarly under another tree and waiting for prayer time. Like us, they all have hijabs over their heads and necks. Some are dressed in long, flowing *abayas* and others are wrapped in layers of cloth. The women are chatting merrily among themselves. The girl and I do not speak to each other.

It is very hot at this time of the year. The rains are at least two months away and the skies are cloudless. The sun beats down mercilessly as the traders, like soldier ants, continue setting out their wares regardless.

I suddenly realise my throat is parched and longingly contemplate the wheelbarrows, full of sachets in ice blocks, being positioned by pure-water sellers. For half a second, I think about going to buy a sachet to salve my thirst but quickly kill the thought—I do not trust myself to be haggling with anyone at this time.

"I want water." The girl startles me. She has suddenly spoken, having obviously followed my gaze. Her voice is low. "But I have no money."

I shrug in sympathy but do not speak.

"My name is Zafira," she persists, speaking under her breath. "What is your name?"

I make to speak but something in her eyes so unsettles me that I swallow the words like warm *kunu* and hold my peace.

Zafira

Why doesn't she talk to me? I need her words to build a fence between me and this madness in my head. Instead, she looks at me with…contempt?

Does she know?

Banza.

Bastard.

He called me *banza*. They did too. Is that why she won't talk to me? Was she there?

The trucks. I see the trucks again. Driving round and round. Very fast. Raising a big dust cloud that covered the whole place. I thought it was the government people. Their needle hurt me the last time they came. When it entered my arm, I cried out. But Baba consoled me. Baba said the needle would make sure that I did not grow a bad leg like Uncle Nuhu.

Oh, Baba! Please come and wake me up. Come and call me Zizizi like you do and take me in your arms. Tell me I have been dreaming. Tell me, "Baba is here, my daughter, it is alright."

I looked across to you, Baba, for assurance when the trucks stopped and the men started jumping down. But what I saw in your eyes terrified me. The only time I had seen that look before was when you saw baby Kadiza playing with the long, black snake. Nothing like that was happening now. So I wanted to ask you what was wrong, what was making you afraid? It was at that moment, just when I wanted to speak, Baba, that the whole world fell apart.

I saw it, Baba, I saw it all. I *saw* the noise. The confusion. The panic. The terror. But I did not hear anything, Baba. It was as if shock had clamped its hand over my right ear and disbelief had clamped over my left so that I was deaf like Mallam Kurame. But my eyes were open. I wanted to close them, but I couldn't. Fear seized my eyelids and held them open so that I saw everything.

You are shouting at me to stay here by the trees, Baba. I cannot hear your voice, but I can see your words. Your mouth is moving rapidly. Your face is close to mine, and your hands grip my shoulders. Your fingers hurt, digging into my skin. There is fire in your eyes, they are open wide, they seem to be swimming inside the rivers of sweat on your face. I see saliva flying from your mouth.

Then you are running, into the smoke and dust, into the madness. Where are you going, Baba? To our *bukka?* To Mama and Kadiza? And then I don't see you again! Baba? Baba?

I might have stood there, transfixed as I was, Baba, until perhaps the horror took me too, but Uncle Nuhu materialised suddenly, from nowhere, and grabbed me by the hand.

He is dragging me towards the bushes. Uncle Nuhu is trying to run but that leg cannot carry him. So he is hobbling and urging me to run. But my legs refuse, Baba. I want to lift them, but they won't obey me. So I am just stumbling along, slower than Uncle Nuhu even.

Uncle Nuhu pulls up abruptly and I stagger into him. One of the men, dressed in black, is blocking our path. Uncle Nuhu is trying to push me behind him. He raises his stick above his head as if he is going to strike the man. But next thing, he falls. Just like that. I look down at him.

He is lying on his stomach. His head is sideways on the ground. Is he suddenly asleep? But his eyes are wide open. Is he playing with the man? Or begging him? I feel a kind of wetness around my feet before I see it, even though I am looking down. There is a dark puddle spreading out from under Uncle Nuhu.

"*Banza.*"

It was the first thing my ears heard since all this started. His voice seemed as if it was coming from very far away, although the man was standing right in front of me, above Uncle Nuhu's body.

"*Banza.*"

I must stop now. I don't want to remember what is coming next. Maybe if I squeeze my eyes shut, I can block it out.

"God is great! God is great! God is great!"

The familiar cry pierces my consciousness, cutting through the cacophony of my thoughts. I open my eyes. People are starting to make their way towards the house of worship. The call to prayer is ringing out.

"There is no god except the one God!"

I realise she is standing, the woman who will not talk to me. She leans down.

"My name is Amina," she whispers. "Look for me in paradise."

And then she is gone, gliding towards the building, her wrappers pulled around her like a shroud.

I try to fix my whole mind on the receding figure, but my thoughts are already rushing back with a vengeance, a cruel wave of torment washing over me, drowning the bustle around me.

Their laughter was raucous. I hear it again as if it is coming through the loudspeakers. I can't even hear the call to prayer anymore. Just their laughter. Like hyenas. And my nostrils are immediately filled with that smell. The smell of their foulness.

At first, I cried and begged for them to stop but that only made them hit me more and kick dust into my face. One after another, over and over, they forced themselves on me and had their way.

My virginity is violently taken from me many times this night. I am bleeding from between my legs. I am bleeding from my back where the stones and sand are inflicting a thousand cuts as the men hold me down, pummel me, and drag me around. I bleed everywhere. There is blood in my eyes, and sand, and dust. But they don't care.

Every time I thought it was over, another would come and remove his trousers, and the pain and torment would start again. By morning, I wished for death. And then the man brought the vest.

Umaru

"*Sannu da aiki*," the woman greets, thanking me for my work. I like that. Who doesn't?

"*Sannu kadai*," I answer, but I don't want to pay her too much attention.

I am scanning all the women approaching with my eyes. The call to prayer has gone out and their numbers are rising rapidly. I detest this cement wall around the house of worship. It has not been long since they built it. It is an ugly wall, an abomination, *abun*. But I understand why they put it here. So that all these people are forced to line up to enter, as they are doing now.

I am standing beside a small gap in the wall. If you pass through the gap, it is but a short walk to the women's section of the building. Everybody says that a gate will be put in the gap, but no one knows when. For now, I am the gate.

"*Salaam alaikum*," one woman says.

"*Alaikum salaam*," I reply, wishing peace unto her in return.

I have been a hunter for as long as I can remember. As soon as I could walk, my father took me hunting in the forest just like his own father had done with him. And so shall it be with my sons. I cannot see why a man would want to live any other way. That is, apart from one thing.

Mata. Women.

They have always fascinated me. Whenever I see a beautiful woman, I find it difficult to breathe. My heart starts to make *jigi-jigi* like *jirgin kasa*, the railway train. But I am a hunter, a creature of the forest. Their world is not there. The way we dress—so that we become one with our habitat—does everything but enamour them of us.

That is why, no matter how many times it has been asked of me to come here and do this work, I find strange the attention of so many women, even if fleeting and forced. Yet it brings me much pleasure and ignites fire in my loins. It would have been a thing of unbridled enjoyment if not for why I am here.

"*Kana lafiya?*" one of the women says, asking how I am doing. Her voice is clear and sweet, the words slipping sonorously off her tongue.

"*Lafiya lau*," I reply, assuring her I am fine. I nod to indicate that she and her companion should enter.

"*Yaya matanka!*" exclaims the companion as they pass me. She is asking about my wife.

I saw the playfulness in their eyes. They are about my age and being mischievous, guessing I am not married. I shake my head as much to clear it as to dismiss these *mami wata*. I have to stop this. I have to be careful.

The thing is, I am sure of where I stand with the wild animals we hunt in the bush. Their first reaction, always, is to flee. But the ones I am looking out for here? *Babu.* They look death in the face and smile and say, "Welcome." And it is difficult to know them until it is too late.

Only by the will of the Almighty, the Merciful and the Beneficent, have a few been stopped in time. When their hijabs were removed, everyone saw that their hair was pulled back tight and tied at the back. Usually, you will only see hair done like that when *mai aikatawa* is preparing a woman's corpse for burial.

"*Sannu.*"

"*Sannu,*" I reply, forcing my mind back to the task at hand.

"*Ina so'n ka,*" she purrs, as she passes.

I shake my head. She said she likes me. The black *kwalli* lining her eyes made her look almost mystical. My heart makes *jigi-jigi* a bit before I order it to stop.

"*Na gode,*" I remember to say, thanking her, but not bothering to turn back.

The worshippers, especially these young women teasing me to distraction, do not behave as if anything is wrong, but that is how our people are. They just continue to live their lives. Everything that happens, good or bad, it is the will of the Almighty.

But all of them know full well why it has been thought fit to bring us here. *Yan sanda,* the police, have not been able to cope, leaving empty stations which—like the policemen themselves—have been frequent targets of the fighters. The government has called out the army and sent them into the bush where the fighters hide, but it is like chasing ghosts.

The fighters, they attack without warning, visiting death and desolation on any village they happen upon. Before the soldiers can even finish pulling on their boots, the fighters have disappeared again like the mirage they say men see when caravans have journeyed far into the desert. And that is why the soldiers are sometimes frustrated and take out their anger on the same *talakawa* that the fighters have just terrorised.

The people have no choice but to fend for themselves, but I still think it a mistake to have us hunters come to *gidan bauta* on *Jummah* to guard them. Even our amulets have no strength here. If you ask me, we are more useful to the cause as the soldiers' eyes and ears in the bush.

I'm looking across at the other hunter with me. His name is Yakubu. He grunts all the time. Some hunters are like that— they have become so used to making the animal and bird sounds that we communicate with in the bush that they can no longer talk properly.

"*Sannu*," a woman greets.

"Arrungh," Yakubu replies, eliciting a loud hiss.

Doing what the soldiers call a "body search" is forbidden to us. We cannot touch a woman who is not our wife, sister or mother. Yes, we can use our guns to order any woman we suspect to step to one side. The question that I keep asking myself is, "What then?" We cannot just shoot anyone we suspect, but if our suspicion is right, we have probably sealed our own fate.

The women are all covered up from head to toe for prayers. Only their faces are visible. It is of no use to look at their stomachs. The way wrappers and *abayas* flow makes it impossible to know if there is a vest underneath. Instead, we search for other telling signs, such as in their gait or mannerism. But even those, of what use are they really? Women are strange. They don't always walk, talk or act normal. Even I know that.

"*Sannu, sannu. Sannu da zuwa.*"

There are three or four lines now, side by side, in front of us and they each stretch a dozen or more back. We do not have a long time to look at each woman before allowing her to enter.

"*Sannu. Barka da rana.*"

I am letting in a mother and daughter when a figure, joining the lines from the across square, catches my attention. She is alone and staring straight ahead, as if in a trance. She cannot be more than sixteen years old, which is two years younger than me. Her arms are invisible under her shawl. My gun starts to rise, almost by itself.

Amina

My eyes are fixed on the entrance to the women's section. Each step brings me closer and closer. And then it hits me. *Rago!* The ram being sacrificed for Eid. The look in its eyes as it is held down, just before its throat is slit. It is a look of resignation yet also of hatred in the utmost, transmitting to executioner and spectator alike a silent but indelible curse. That was what I saw in Zafira's eyes.

I should really have spoken to the poor girl. And assured her that whatever has brought her here, whatever has happened to her, is the will of the Almighty.

Indeed, what was it if not the will of the Almighty that brought the fighters into our *kauye*? If not that He willed it, I would not have beheld people I loved being butchered. Did she ever see her grandmother burn as I saw my *kaka*, twisting and wailing in agony, as the flames consumed her? That was the Almighty's will too.

I was rounded up with other young women and forced into a ditch. I am not sure I have the words to describe enough our terror at thinking we would be buried alive. That was until the fighters started sharing us among themselves. Many of us refused to leave the ditch, but they brought six men we knew—brothers, uncles, fathers and friends—and slit their throats by the ditch, the blood spurting at first, then gushing into the ditch until we were standing in a pool of muddy blood.

"If you refuse to marry, this is what will happen to you!"

So I became the wife of Farouk, one of them. How I hated him, and all of them, at first, with a fury I never knew possible. Then, after three months in the bush with him, I found myself, to my dismay, starting to look forward to when Farouk would come to me. By the fifth month, he was my life.

My happiness was willed to last until the day the soldiers stormed the camp. There was no way they could have found that camp if they were not with the hunters. Even as the shooting, shouting and stampeding was happening, I wondered whether it was the same hunters who brought meat to sell to us as we changed camps. I wanted to run with Farouk, but it was not the Almighty's will—I was heavy with child. I do not know what became of him. The soldiers took me and other women home.

I was overjoyed to see my father and the other members of the family that survived. But my heart ached for Farouk. I missed him in a way I could never have imagined possible for another human being. At the same time, I felt guilty, first for missing him and then for having to hide it from everyone else, especially after their initial welcome turned cold.

People, my own family, fa, looked at me with scorn and spat in my direction as I passed. My surprise and confusion quickly gave way to sorrow and pain. And then I was seized with an unspeakable rage.

The birth salved my soul, but it was only to be short-lived. I had to bury my beautiful *mala'ika* alone in the bush away from the village. Even my father, Uba, of all people, praised God that the "devil child"—*dan shaidan*—died five days after he came into the world.

I listened and listened to rumours of where the fighters might be and eventually I ran, in the middle of the night, and ran and ran until I found them. And then it was *I* who told them I wanted a vest.

All that was His will, the same will that brought me here. Now, I must join the queue. And then it is just a matter of time.

The sight of the hunters by the wall rips the scabs off a wound inside me. Their hideous attire will always give them away. See the one on this side of the queue. Could he be one of those that came with the soldiers to the camp? Wait. He is staring at me? I must…

"*Menene*!" What?

A pregnant woman is challenging the other man, the one who looks like a gorilla. He is pointing at her distended belly.

"*Menene wannan*!" She is waving her hands in his face. I feel an instant kinship with her.

The man swings his gun above his shoulder. He is trying to make her back off by jabbing the butt in the air in her direction. It is not even a serious gun, not like the AK that Farouk taught me to fire. I hiss inwardly.

The young hunter hesitates, looking from the commotion to me and back again. He steps across to intervene.

Everybody in the queue is taking advantage of the distraction to bypass the guards, and this brings me quicker than I had expected to the entrance. The hunter who was looking at me is still entangled in the melee. I walk past them into the premises.

"Woman, stop. Wait. Stop. You."

There is a mass of women here, but I know it is to me that the male voice is addressed. For a moment I think about doing it now, but I change my mind and turn. As I expected, it is the young hunter. He is standing just inside the wall now and pointing the gun, held by the barrel with one hand, at me.

"Yes, you," he says, beckoning with the gun. "Please come back."

He should be about the same age as Farouk, no longer a boy but not yet a man. Even here, even now, my heart aches for Farouk.

I start to walk back, with my eyes on the ground. Only when I am a few steps from him do I raise my head. There is a smile on my face. I hope it is a triumphant one. I need only one hand for what I am about to do. So I free my left hand and use it to sweep back my hijab and the scarf under, revealing my hairdo.

He drops the gun in shock. I laugh. As he struggles, fumbling to pick up the gun, I proclaim the greatness of the Creator and push the plunger with all my might.

Mukhtar

The events across the square are much to my liking. Everything there is shrouded in smoke and dust. This is the part I like best, immediately after, when everyone is stupefied.

"*Menene wancan? Menene? Menene?*" What is that? What happened?

"*Ban sani ba!*" No one is sure.

"*Wuta! Wuta!*" There is fire.

"*Nakiya! Nakiya!*" It was an explosion

I am pleased but not entirely. The explosion went off as prayers were about to start which is what I desired. But I wanted it inside. Something happened at the gate with the girl. I saw a scuffle. Maybe she was found out.

Still, there seems to be considerable devastation. The blast shattered the glass in the building; I saw a shower of shards in the big fire cloud. Imagine the effect inside the building. Praise be to the Almighty!

Cries for help are starting to rent the air.

"*Taimako! Taimako!*"

The police are also being sought.

"*Kira yan sanda! Kira yan sanda!*"

This, my fifth bombing, should be my most successful. The highest tally I have so far is about forty, by the third bombing, at Madalla. Everybody knows I did that with Kabiru. This one is mine, and mine alone.

Sirens already? *Walahi*, they are learning. Before, it would take an hour before anything resembling an ambulance showed face. But this is good because, in a short while, the crowd here will be bigger than even before the explosion. It is then that they will see my hand and the power of the Creator, the Exalted in Might—a second bombing, deadlier than the first.

A smile lights my face. There is definitely a new record in the making.

I can see the other girl from here. She is still sitting under the mango tree as if nothing is happening around her. I keep an eye on her as I film everything on my phone. As the minutes pass, quite a crowd gathers, including the assortment of uniforms I wanted. The time is ripe.

She gets up as if on my signal. Her instincts are perfect. May the Almighty, the Superior, the Bestower of Faith, be praised. But what, now? She is looking around as if she is unsure where to go.

Banza!

Ah, okay, she starts tracing the footsteps of the first one, walking slowly towards the square. Thanks be to the Almighty. That is all I needed to see.

My spirit deems it unwise to tarry. Too many *dan doka,* people of the law, are gathering. Who knows what Kabiru told them about us when he was being tortured? Foolish boy. He allowed our exploits get into his head and became careless. I shall not be apprehended like a dog as he was. In the house of a whore, fa. *Dan boroba shegey!* I conjure up the phlegm in my throat and spit it out.

I make my way through overturned stalls and animated people, into the tangle of three-wheel *kekes* parked beyond the market. I have my own *keke,* the taxi of the masses. Driving it is the perfect camouflage when I come into town. I can transport my *wakilin mutuwa,* my angels of death, like the second girl today, without arousing suspicion.

The park is in tumult and shrouded in dust. Drivers are revving their engines, trying to extricate themselves from gridlock.

"*A lura sosai! A lura sosai!*" Look out! Look out!

"*Ba hanya!*" No way through!

"*Tsaya! Dakata!*" Stop! Wait!

"*Dan boroba! Dan banza! Shegey!*" Bastards.

People with hideous injuries are being brought up to be ferried to hospital.

"*Taimako! Taimako!*" Help! Help!

I feel giddy with excitement at the sight of blood and shattered bodies on makeshift stretchers. This is my work, my accomplishment. The Almighty be praised, I say over and over as I adjust my turban to cover my nose and mouth against the dust.

I have no sympathy whatsoever for these people. They are apostates, *ridda,* who have blasphemed, despicably, by the way they live. They deserve the worst death possible, and I am bringing it to them.

I video some more as I walk to where my *keke* is parked. If I add religious chanting before putting it online, it will be more dramatic. I know exactly which cleric to conscript. The one-eyed, old fool will be of better use there than spending his time marrying off girls to fighters. *Dan boroba*—such a waste of potential bombers. I wish my brothers would keep their loins under control. Or even seek the simpler comforts of a fellow man.

I post my videos as "Sheikh Nakiya," a name that acclaims me the king of explosions. My standing in the ranks of fighters has grown with each posting, so much so, I have been told, that no less than Abu Bakr Shiku, the Darul Tawheed, speaks my name with respect. The way I am going, Sheikh Nakiya shall one day, as the Almighty wills it, become the leader of the People of the Proper Way of Life, Committed to Proselytising and Holy Struggle. I hate the name of derision that infidels call us. May I die a thousand deaths before my lips utter that perfidy.

I get to the *keke* and set my bag down. Despite the chaos, my access to the main road is open. It is as I envisaged. I am hemmed in at the back and sides but can drive straight out onto the road.

I am about to put the key in the ignition when I sense a figure stopping in front of the vehicle. I look up. The dust obscures my sight a bit, but I think it is a woman. She probably thinks I am available for hire. I wave my hands to indicate that I am not interested. She does not move.

"*Tafi daga nan!*" I shout at her to go away.

She still does not move.

I order her again. "*Gafara dai! Bar nan!*"

I am infuriated. The foolish woman must still be in shock at the bombing. I pull out my dagger. *Walahi*, I will send this *wawa* to meet her Maker now. Then a thought strikes me. Perhaps she can be my next recruit. I grin broadly, my anger disappearing like smoke exhaled in the wind of the Sahel.

I put a foot on the ground, sheathing the blade, and lean out so I can beckon her to come closer. Only then do I see her well.

It is the second girl. What is she doing here when…?

I see a movement under her *abaya*.

Bismillah.

THE INTERVIEW

"What is your name?"

The woman in the booth usually started with this question. It was hard to believe how many of them were caught out when asked to state their names. She folded her arms across her bosom and reared back on her swivel chair to regard the applicant on the other side of the glass.

"Chineze Nwankwo."

Chineze was annoyed. The woman was looking at her like a criminal. She probably believed the country was full of morons who did not know their names.

"Which is the surname? That is, your family name?"

"Nwankwo is my surname. It is there on the form in front of you."

Having spat out the words, Chineze grudgingly admitted to herself that the woman was not entirely out of order. Nowadays, people here mixed up given names and surnames, confusing foreigners who were used to a certain sequence. At the urging of pastors—those ubiquitous "men and women of God"—it had also become fashionable to take up names that supposedly spoke to one's aspirations. "Proclaiming your destiny," they called it. People with normal names like "Chineze Nwankwo" would therefore suddenly become "Prosper Godsfavour."

"Okay, so what would you have me call you? May I call you Chineze?"

The clashing consonants of their names had initially challenged the woman, but now, nine months into the posting, it was a "small matter," as they liked to say. She'd discovered a gift for languages when she took Mandarin in high school. By the time she hit the "send" button on her application to the State Department, she had also become fluent in Portuguese and French, despite never having set foot outside Arkansas.

"That's alright. Chineze is fine."

Chineze had wanted to say, "You can call me whatever you like," but was surprised at how well the woman pronounced "Chee-nay-zay." Usually when they were looking at it in writing as this woman was, they went for "Chai-neez" even after she had said it properly to them.

"Oh, good. Thank you. Now tell me, Chineze, why do you want to go to the United States?"

The woman skimmed through the application. She detached a card—a wedding invitation—from the form. It was a beautiful card, the kind she hoped she would have whenever she got married. She looked at the back of the card and took note of the company that made it.

"My uncle is getting married in Baltimore, and I'm going to be a bridesmaid. It's on the form."

"I see. . ."

They liked nice things, these people; you couldn't take that away from them. Which was why the woman found it difficult to comprehend their inability to fix a country sorely in need of a makeover, starting with the crater-like potholes outside the embassy. She wrinkled her nose, reflexively.

"Sorry, is there any problem?"

Chineze wondered why the foolish woman was turning up her nose at the card and even scrutinising the little print at the back. Did she think it was fake?

"Just a minute, Chineze, I'm *juuust* looking at some of your documents here."

The woman hoped the invitation was real. They would spare no cost to fake anything—card, ceremony, sibling and all—for the sake of a visa. There were many qualities she admired in them, such as their tenacity and zest for life, but their unparalleled dishonesty was not one.

"Ah, okay."

"Your uncle's surname is Uwakwe? That's not your surname?"

It was another trick the woman liked to try. You followed up a question with one that was the same but worded differently and then got an answer that contradicted the first.

"No, he's my mother's youngest brother. My mother's family name is Uwakwe."

"So your mother is Mrs. Uwakwe?"

"No, she's Mrs. Nwankwo. Her maiden name was Uwakwe."

"I see."

So far so good, although you could never be sure. Little old la-dies—grandmas—had sat where Chineze now did and lied through their teeth. Their "visa agents"—touts by any other name—schooled them, paying scant regard to the fact that the consular officers had heard it all before. The woman wrinkled her nose again.

"Is there anything you want me to explain?"

Chineze wished the woman would stop doing that funny thing with her nose—it made her look ugly. And who told young white women in America anyway that a nasal voice, the "valley girl" accent many of them affected, was cool or sexy? The woman sounded like a robot sorely in need of a battery recharge.

"I will ask the questions, okay?"

The woman kept her voice firm and—she hoped—her mien inscrutable. She had all the power in this fleeting relationship and would shortly wield it according to her fancy. Applicants came in here nervous and ingratiating, knowing that going to America, their El Dorado, depended on interviewers like her. Only if the visa was refused did the sheep's clothing come off. Then, security often had to be called to stop them shouting, "Do you know who I am?"

"Okay, sorry, *ma'am.*

"That's alright."

Few, very few, were forward from the outset like Chineze, who had tinged even the "ma'am" with sarcasm. Still, in the woman's ex-perience, the feistiness was affected. Once the applicant was caught out in a lie or two, groveling took over. It was coming with Chineze. The woman was sure.

"Right, let's go on to a few questions about you, Chineze."

"Okay, ma'am."

Chineze could not believe the nerve of the woman—what was she smirking for? She wished she could reach across the glass and pull the woman's cheeks, like you did with rude little girls. Look at her, she thought, common consular officer, behaving if she were the ambassador himself.

"Have you been refused a US visa before?"

The woman stared at Chineze again. She knew that people rarely looked each other in the eyes in these parts. The woman could not recall how many applicants she had unsettled with an unblinking gaze.

"No. I've never applied before. This is my first time."

"So you've never been to the United States?"

The woman acknowledged that the applicant spoke English well, with the slightest hint of an American accent. She had been surprised when she first came out here at the reach of American culture, and she'd been even more surprised at how they had appropriated it, like the rapping in Pidgin English, which she loved.

"No. I've never been. I said so on the form."

Chineze had thought about replying in the affirmative, to tell the woman that Chineze Nwankwo had been to—no, *in*—America ever since she could comprehend things. There was no escaping the America that was all around her, every day, on DSTV, social media, everywhere.

She knew all the stars and the gossip, could hold court on the best shops on Rodeo Drive or where to catch a bite on Fifth Avenue, and was convinced she knew who shot JFK, 2Pac and Biggie.

The serious stuff too—the history and the geography, the politics and the wars—were par for the course. She knew them better than she knew the same about her country. So, yes, she had been to "Stets" as traders from the East called it. And she would bet her last dollar that she knew America better than this nasal woman "forming American" across the glass from her.

"I do not see your bank statements here?"

The woman stopped herself from chuckling. She had Chineze in her crosshairs now.

"No. I didn't submit any."

"Why not?"

"Because I don't have a bank account."

"You don't have a bank account, Chineze?"

"No, I don't. I just told you so."

"But you do know, *ma'am,* that your account statements are one of the main things we request when you apply for a visa?"

The woman in the booth smiled. She was being condescending, but Chineze's naivety justified that. The savvy ones tendered bogus papers if they did not have anything that passed muster. It was difficult to run checks in a country without databases. To make matters worse, the scale of forgery here was beyond compare.

"Yes, I do know that."

"And you honestly want me to believe that you don't have a bank account?"

There was a place—Oluwole they called it. A few of the consulate staff had visited once, out of curiosity, posing as tourists on a Saturday walkabout. Shop runners fawned over them in dim and squalid warrens, where document makers and engravers toiled away, unmindful of scrutiny by strangers. One engaging old man with globular eyes had even followed the woman about, offering "*genue* passport, any country, for married or single."

"I don't have a bank account. My father gave me a debit card on one of his accounts. That's how I pay my way."

"Really, Chineze?"

The woman had cottoned on to the proper pronunciation, "Oloo-Woh-LAY," as against the Consul General's insistence on "Olieu-Wall." Some of the work from the place was crude, but in the main, the craftsmanship was impressive. Once, an applicant had tendered a letter signed by the ambassador. Poor Mr. Brinkley. It had taken the good ol' Texan, and his thick glasses, ten minutes of poring over the document—with the concerned visa officer stifling a laugh—before he could be sure it wasn't him that had signed it.

"Really, ma'am."

"You don't have any proof of means whatsoever to give us?"

Something about Oluwole reminded the woman of Canal Street in New York. She could never get over NYPD's finest patrolling the area while turning a blind eye to the hawking of counterfeit goods. At first it had been just Chinese sellers, but now Africans, Senegalese especially, were crawling the sidewalks. And then there were the tourist hordes from all over the world—the cheek of it—trying in full view to snag replica LV bags or Chanel sunglasses as mementos of their time in the Big Apple.

"No, but I can't give you what I don't have, can I? Maybe you would have preferred it if I'd brought something from Oluwole, yes?"

Chineze did not think the woman would know what or who she was talking about, but she did not care. These visa officers surely left the embassy's gilded quarters rarely, and then only to mingle with fellow *oyibo* in the boat clubs and luxury apartments on the island that were their preserve. She knew many people who had obtained visas and green cards with bogus papers. The Americans thought they were all that, but illiterate forgers who could not even speak proper English were deceiving them every day.

"Again, Chineze, I must remind you that I do the asking."

"Okay, sorry. I was just…anyway, sorry."

Serves you all right, Chineze thought, being as pompous as this woman. Still, Chineze disdained Oluwole. Could the new governor of the state, a self-styled "action man," hurry up with closing the place now that it had been a minute from when he made the campaign promise?

"So if you don't have any money, how will you maintain yourself in America? I see you want to stay for three weeks after the wedding?"

"My uncle will take care of me."

"He paid for your ticket, I see?"

The woman extracted the Delta Airlines printout. It seemed genuine, although it was not a mandatory requirement for the visa application. Comfort Plus seating? The alleged uncle was obviously doing better stateside than average.

"Yes, he did."

"And what does your uncle do?"

"He's a doctor at Johns Hopkins."

"You mean John Hopkins?"

"No. *Johns* Hopkins. The hospital in Baltimore."

There you go. The woman did not even know the proper name of one of America's most famous hospitals. Chineze would have a proper laugh about it with her uncle when next they spoke.

"Aha, right. I see. And what does he do there?"

The woman had looked up Dr. Jideofor Uwakwe on the Johns Hopkins website as they'd spoken and been impressed. Associate professor of neurology and neuroscience who published a lot of papers. Whatever "nucleocytoplasmic transport in C9orf72-mediated ALS/FTD" meant, he seemed to be quite the expert in it.

"I just said he was a doctor there, didn't I?"

"Miss Nwankwo—"

"Sorry...I—"

"Let me finish. If this happens again, I will end this interview immediately. Do you understand me?"

"Yes, I'm sorry, ma'am."

"Where was I? Yes, did your uncle go to med school in America?"

"No, he studied medicine here."

"So how did he get to settle in America?"

He must have gone on a tourist visa, the woman hazarded, and then contracted a sham marriage that had been dissolved as soon as he got residency. She had seen an old movie about it, *Green Card*, starring the Frenchman, Depardieu, opposite one of Hollywood's darlings of the nineties. Admittedly, the film also proved that these people were not the only ones given to the scam.

"He won the green-card lottery from here."

Chineze was pleased to rebut any notions the woman might have about her uncle marrying for papers.

"Oh, I see. The Diversity Visa Program?"

One of the lucky ones, the woman thought. OMG, how she hated the foreigners who abused immigration rules, especially since she'd started working at the State Department and had seen the scale of it.

"Yes."

Chineze regretted not bringing anything warmer than a light sweater. The air conditioning inside the consulate was legendary.

OMG, if she did not know better, she would think they wanted to give visa hopefuls a feel of winter conditions in places like Minneapolis. Or perhaps it was just another of their devices to discomfit applicants. The contrast to the tropical heat outside could not be starker.

"Has he been married before?"

"No. He hasn't."

"So, this is his first marriage?"

The new president promised to make America great again. The woman willed him to tighten the rules that let in dishonest people from places like this but could not get them out. She shuddered to think what would happen to the American way of life if enough of them got in.

"Yes, it is his first marriage, but I thought I just told you…"

"You just told me what, Chineze?"

"Nothing, ma'am. Nothing."

"Okay, so back to you, Chineze. You don't have any letter from an employer?"

"No."

"Do you have a job?"

"No. I just graduated from uni—from college. I'm yet to do national service, so no job yet."

"Are you married?"

The woman glanced at Chineze's unadorned fingers. Perhaps she was still too young at twenty. Her earrings were nice though, the woman thought, as she looked the applicant in the eye again.

"No."

"Never married?"

"Never."

Chineze saw that the woman had no wedding band. Perhaps the thing with the nose put off men, or women—you could never tell these days. But the woman's earrings were nice. Silver and bold, they had an elegant script that Chineze could not make out. Not Fendi, probably Tiffany. Chineze made a mental note to search for them online later.

"Do you own any real estate? You know—land, buildings?"

"No."

"So let me get this straight, Chineze, you don't have a job, you're not married, and you don't own any real estate?"

"Yes."

"Yes you do, or no you don't?"

"No, I don't."

Chineze considered the grammar lesson rich, coming from valley girl here from the land of double negatives. She wondered what the woman would have said if she had answered in her best imitation of a Southern drawl, "No, ma'am, I ain't got no property."

"Did you read the guidance on applying for a visa?"

This was becoming strange. Chineze had to have a story coming, some plea of exculpation that was probably a hoax.

"Yes, some of it."

"Just some of it?"

"Yes, it was quite long."

Chineze smiled. Everyone she knew could recite, offhand, the requirements for an American visa. She did not need to bore herself with reading the embassy's guidance to prepare for the interview.

"Well, did you read enough of it to know that we require proof that you have sufficient ties to your home country to bring you back?"

"I guess so."

"And you do know that you have provided me with nothing to show that you intend to return if I grant you a visa?"

"Well, I gave you what I have. At least that's the whole truth right there. If what I have is not enough, that's fine. It's not the end of the world."

Chineze smiled some more. The befuddled look on the woman's face was priceless. The woman had green eyes. Were they natural or contacts? Or laser surgery perhaps, like in those YouTube videos? The woman was striking, actually—if only she could rid herself of the severe expression she'd worn since the interview started.

"Hmm, Chineze, I must say I like your candor; we don't usually get that here. All the same, for me to grant this visa, you must provide me with the basis to grant it. I'm afraid you've not given me a lot to work with."

The woman was perplexed. The applicant fit the profile of someone who would abscond to America at the slightest opportunity. Yet, Chineze carried on as if she genuinely did not care. The woman could not remember seeing one of those in her time here. All of them, old and young, wanted to get to America. It was a status symbol for the wealthy, the Promised Land for the struggling and an obsession for all.

"Sorry, ma'am. That's everything I've got."

The woman regarded her quizzically for a long moment before turning to the application. Chineze was sure this was one of the easiest refusals that the woman would give. As the woman leafed through the documents, scribbling furiously, Chineze began to crave a burger and reflected that it quite fit the irony of the situation. When the woman eventually put her pen down and looked up, Chineze smiled, head cocked.

"Okay, Chineze. I've reviewed your application and have made a decision."

"Which is…?"

"Your visa will be ready in three days."

It was the woman's turn to smile. A strange look had come over Chineze. The woman could not tell whether it was shock or panic, but the cockiness had certainly vanished. Chineze seemed as if she had suddenly folded into herself. The woman was thrilled.

"Wha-what? You're giving me a visa? But…"

"You didn't see that coming, did you?" The woman wanted to laugh.

"No, not at all. But…but why?"

"Why? Well, you seemed to be telling the truth, Chineze. That counts for everything, at least for me. I do hope you will come back."

"Err…yes, of course…but. . ."

"You truly didn't want this visa, did you?" The woman raised an eyebrow.

"No, I didn't."

"You know, I actually believe you. So why did you apply?"

"Well...err...I didn't want to disappoint my family, especially my mother. Uncle Jide. They made me apply for this visa." Chineze sounded apologetic, her voice much softer now than it had been at any time during the interview.

"So now you won't disappoint them. But why do *you* look so disappointed?"

"It's just that...you see...it's like... No. You won't understand?"

"Really? Try me."

The woman leaned back as she had at the start of the interview, folding her arms, but this time there was a grin on her face. She liked Chineze's colour-blocked sweater. It looked like cashmere. The woman wondered how many times Chineze would find the occasion to wear it in the perennially hot weather.

"Okay. Here goes," Chineze began, after a pause. "My boyfriend is coming back from Malaysia next week. He's been away for a year. Master's degree. I miss him like you can't even believe. I wanted to spend time with him when my family travelled for the wedding. You know, one month. Stay at his place, do whatever I want. I just came here to fulfil all righteousness. I honestly didn't think you were going to grant the visa. Does that make sense?"

"Haha, yes it does, Chineze. Woman to woman, believe me it does. Your boyfriend's a lucky man. I hope he knows it. I've granted your visa though. Enjoy the trip if you do decide to go. I'm sure you'll make a lovely bridesmaid."

Once out of the consulate, Chineze picked up the phone and speed-dialed. It was still early in chilly Baltimore, but the voice on the line was bright and cheery.

"What happened, Chi?"

"Uncle, Uncle, it worked! It worked, just as you said, it worked!"

A PROVOCATION

"Cooourt!" the court registrar bellowed as the clock on the wall struck nine.

Everybody sprang to their feet. The Right Honourable the Chief Justice Bola Dada shuffled into view, scowling. Instead of the usual judges' bow, he gave us a sideways lean. He sat down before we emerged from the deep bows that lawyers were obliged to give in return.

It was Monday morning. Lawyers overflowed from our designated seating enclosure to the benches for the public, who in turn spilled out to the corridor outside. We were fully costumed in wigs and gowns, black suits, and peaked collars and bibs, as was required in the high court.

Temperatures were high even at this hour. Our attire, a colonial relic, was ludicrous for the weather. The saving grace was air conditioning that worked, but only because it was the chief judge's court. We would not be so lucky in other courtrooms on the premises. I uttered a prayer against a power cut.

"Call the case for judgment," the chief judge growled.

The court registrar squinted at the cause list and called out, "The State against Lukeman Braimoh."

"Is the accused in court?" The chief judge demanded.

"Yes, my Lord," the registrar confirmed as my client walked into the dock in a smart, pin-striped suit. We had chosen the outfit together, carefully, at the weekend.

"Who is counsel in the matter?" The chief judge was still growling. I hoped it was not a bad omen.

James Oke, the director of public prosecution, stood and announced that he was representing the State. As Mr. Oke sat down, I got up, pulling my gown forwards by the shoulders.

"My Lord, I am Ekpen Seghale, and I appear for the accused."

The chief judge shuffled a pile of papers in front of him and looked at us from under his glasses.

"Here is my judgement."

He started by recounting the facts. The accused, Lukeman Braimoh, was a general manager at First Trust Bank. The accused had come home from work early on the day in question. His son's school had called him to pick up his son who had fallen ill. The school had not been able to reach his wife on the phone.

"When he entered his home, he encountered his wife and the first prosecution witness, Olawale Toriola, whom I shall refer to hereafter as 'PW1,' having sex in the living room."

The chief judge looked up, pausing for effect. Receiving the desired reaction—a murmur from the courtroom—he continued.

"The accused ordered PW1 to dress up and leave. PW1 was also the CEO of First Trust Bank and the accused's direct supervisor at the bank. While putting on his clothes, PW1 asked why the accused was not at work anyway."

Another pause drew another murmur.

"At this stage, from all accounts, the accused lost control and attacked PW1. The second prosecution witness was the accused's wife at the time but is now estranged. She testified that the accused was 'like an animal' and that PW1 'never stood a chance.'"

There was some chuckling. I did not look back, but it had to have come from men.

"The accused tore the clothes off PW1 and pushed him naked outside, locking the door after him. PW1 admitted in cross-examination that he had driven himself to the liaison with the accused's wife so that his chauffeur would not know what he was up to."

More chuckling.

The chief judge looked to the back of the courtroom. Perhaps he was trying to locate Mr. Toriola, PW1, whom I had seen in court earlier.

"Stumbling outside and realising that he did not have his keys, PW1 went back to the front door and started banging on it. PW1, PW2 and the accused concurred in their various testimonies that PW1 uttered words to the effect of 'useless man, c'mon give me my keys—she's not worth losing your job for.'"

The court broke out in laughter.

"Order in court!" the registrar yelled.

Things quickly quietened down, and the judge continued his summary of the testimony.

"The accused opened the door and dealt several punches to PW1, knocking PW1 on the ground. Thereafter, he grabbed a rake lying in the driveway, jumped over PW1 and attacked PW1's car, a Porsche Cayenne. The accused smashed the windows and windshield of the car and destroyed the bodywork before pouring petrol on it and setting it ablaze."

There was an audible gasp in court—such an expensive car gone to waste, just like that.

"While the accused was engaged with the car, PW1 recovered and escaped naked on foot. He sustained a gash on his thigh while scaling the spiked gate of the premises. The accused had locked the gate upon seeing a strange vehicle in the driveway. PW1 made a complaint later that day to the police. The accused was arrested and eventually arraigned."

I smiled at the imagery evoked. PW1's emergence, stark naked, from the accused's compound was the reason why the court was full today. No sooner had he landed outside than phone cameras were clicking and photos were being uploaded on social media. Within an hour, *Linda Ikeji's Blog* published the story, and it went viral. By the end of the day, serious newspapers like *Punch* and *Vanguard* were carrying pictures with headlines such as "Adultery: Bank CEO Caught Naked." Titillating accounts followed for weeks.

"The accused has been charged before this court on seven counts."

My smile turned to a grimace. Matters like this did not usually get to court, the police being wont to side with the cuckolded man. But Mr. Toriola, PW1, was a powerful man, as all bank CEOs were. Infuriated by his public humiliation, he'd pulled all his connections to not only charge the accused but throw the book at him.

Charge number one was for assault, which carried a year's imprisonment. The second charge was for assault occasioning harm, which carried three years. The next charge was for doing grievous bodily harm, punishable with a seven-year sentence. The heavy ones came after that. My client was charged with attempting to do grievous harm with intent to maim, disfigure or disable, a felony which carried imprisonment for life. He was also charged with attempted murder, another felony punishable with life imprisonment.

There were also charges relating to the car. One was for destroying or damaging property, punishable with two years of imprisonment. The other was for arson, a felony for which my client could be jailed for fourteen years.

"The facts are not much in dispute from the evidence," the chief judge asserted. "While testifying, the accused apologised to his wife, PW2, and Mr. Toriola, PW1. He said he acted in the heat of the moment, having been consumed by rage at not only the adultery but PW1's offensive words. He said he lost control and didn't know what he was doing anymore."

I had schooled my client well on how to present his testimony. The teary courtroom apologies were my idea and had taken some suasion. He had protested with vehemence, still bristling at the cuckoldry. Only my reminder of the prospect of life imprisonment at Kirikiri had brought him around.

"The accused's stance amounted to a plea of provocation, which his counsel elaborated upon in closing address."

I permitted myself a broad grin as the chief judge adverted to me. Provocation was my forte. I had made a career of it.

"The criminal code states that assault is an offence unless it is excused by law. One of the instances in which assault is so excused is where there is provocation. A person is not criminally responsible for assault on another who gives him provocation. The provocation must deprive the person of the power of self-control, and he must have acted on it immediately and before there was time for his passion to cool."

Settled law, I mused.

"In this case, the accused comes home and finds another man on top of his wife. To add insult to the injury, the man is his boss and questions him as to why he is not at work. The boss then tells the man that his adulterous wife is not even worth it."

There was laughter which the registrar quelled with another shout of "Order!"

"Few things can reasonably provoke a man more than another caught in *flagrante delicto* committing adultery with his wife. Yet, the accused kept his cool and demanded that PW1 leave. The accused only lost control after PW1 made remarks that I think, in all honesty, most men of personable comportment would find insulting even at the best of times. Those remarks, in this case, constituted the last straw for the accused."

As I'd anticipated, the chief judge was taking a dim view of PW1's aggravating conduct. I had deployed all my goodwill with the chief registrar of the high court to ensure that the case was assigned to the chief judge's court. If our CEO of a PW1 thought he was the only one with influence, he had another think coming. The case could have gone to any other court, but there was a reason I'd wanted it here at all costs.

The chief judge was a lifelong bachelor. He had been cuckolded as a young lawyer, his fiancée becoming pregnant after cheating with the principal of the firm in which he worked. It was a well-kept secret. I would never have known if I had not heard it from the master of my masonic lodge, who had happened to work in the same firm at the time. It was one of those nuggets of information that you keep close to your chest and think nothing of, until one day it becomes quite significant.

"I have looked at the elements of provocation, and I find that all of them exist in the accused's favour in this case."

"As the court pleases," resounded in court. That was the customary refrain when a judge announced a finding.

"I find that the gravity of the provocation caused the accused to lose control and he acted in the heat of passion. I do not see anything in the evidence suggesting that the force the accused used was disproportionate to the provocation."

"As the court pleases!"

"PW1's medical report was tendered as Exhibit 2. There is nothing in it that shows any grievous harm done by the accused to PW1.

Indeed, the only thing in the report approaching grievous bodily harm, as defined by the code, was the injury that PW1 sustained as he climbed over the gate."

The chief judge's voice remained gravelly, but it was paving the path to my client's freedom.

"I do not see anything in the evidence suggesting that the accused intended to cause death or grievous harm. I agree with learned counsel for the defence that if the accused had intended to kill, maim or otherwise cause grievous harm to PW1, he would have hit PW1 with the rake while PW1 was prostrate on the ground. Instead, the accused jumped over PW1."

My closing address had hammered on the point about the rake. The ship of defence was in sight of port.

"As for damage to the car, the code says it is lawful for any person to use such force as is necessary to prevent the repetition of an act or insult which is such as to be provocation to him for an assault. The accused testified that he vented his fury on the car because it was PW1's conveyance to the accused's home and therefore symbolic of the adultery. I find that the destruction of the car resulted directly from provocation, the accused acting in the heat of passion and without there being time for the passion to cool."

"As the court pleases!" We were practically home and dry.

"Accordingly, I find the accused not guilty of any of the charges. I hereby discharge and acquit the accused on all seven counts."

"As the court pleases!"

Applause broke out from the accused's supporters. I looked at the dock. My client was pumping his fists and dancing what seemed like *shaku shaku*.

"The case is dismissed. Mr. Braimoh, you are now a free man. Please step out of the dock."

I gathered my files while my learned colleagues leaned over to shake my hand or pat me on the shoulders. The Provoke King had done it again.

As I leave court on the owner's seat in my Range Rover, I think about how far this Edo boy has come in two decades of law practice. Yes, there are the sumptuous residences in Lagos and London, but my pride and joy is the palatial mansion I completed last year in Igueben, my home town. It is worthy to mention, of course, the library, dormitories, and principal's office that were refurbished, single-handed, at Igueben Grammar School within the year. One must give back, I think, lest providence turn its back on one so richly blessed.

Vivian, my darling wife, does not work, as befits a spouse of the well-heeled. She spends her days with ladies who lunch and compare jewelry on Banana Island—that is, when they are not shopping around the world, with stopovers to visit the children in school in England.

I have a son at Eton, which you must know is where Princes William and Harry went. The other son is at the London Oratory, which is where Tony Blair's son studied. I have plans to send them to university in America—Harvard or Yale, preferably.

I am happy with the life I live. It was all down to one incident, years ago.

My family was not rich. I was working as a shop assistant, putting myself through law school at the time. The only means of transport I could afford was the molue bus. Permit me a brief digression to describe this icon of our dystopian traffic to you.

In shape and size, the molue resembles the buses Americans send their children to school in. It even has the same colours, yellow and black, as its American cousin, but that is where the similarities end. Air conditioning? No, *iro ni,* never for the molue. Legroom? British people would say "you're having a laugh, mate," but we'll just leave it at affirming that maximum capacity and the molue did not exist in the same universe.

But don't get me wrong, the molue is dearly beloved of our poor and boisterous masses. They need no telling that without it, they would probably have no means to traverse this unforgiving megapolis of great expectations and crushed dreams.

Molue drivers are driven people and no, I do not mean that as a pun. You see, the molue driver does not usually own his vehicle. He has hired it on the understanding he pays the owner a certain amount every day in addition to covering the vehicle's running costs. This arrangement, as you can imagine, makes molue drivers drive like their lives depend on the next fare.

Anyway, on the day of the incident, I was going from Oshodi to law school. As things turned out, it was my good fortune to be seated in front, where I could see the driver. I was one of the first on the bus as it started its journey, owing to my youth and agility at the time.

A molue does not come to a halt at bus stops. It merely slows down. Once it comes into sight, the waiting throng must set off like relay runners in the direction in which the bus is headed. The trick is to time the bus so that as its door comes abreast, you jump on quick enough to grasp the handlebar and haul yourself in. There are no second chances. You have to get it right the first time, for your own good and out of courtesy for the person behind you in the relay.

The driver on the day, as I would learn, was "Baba Ibeji" which means "father of twins." He wore a towel around his neck and no shirt, his rickety upper body ballooning into the kind of bulbous tummy inevitable for one who sat hunched over all day. He had on a *sokoto*—the traditional trousers—in cheap lace fabric. He was not an imposing man, but he maneuvered that behemoth in and out of traffic with unerring dexterity, hauling the flat steering wheel around like one engaged in a wrestling match with a python.

Shortly after we left Oshodi, however, we encountered the first of the many uniforms which assail commercial transportation in the city. Everyone knows them by their colours—gold and red in this case, the traffic management authority. One of their number executed the running hop onto the front door.

"Settle your man, let me be going," he said to the driver, hanging half in and half out of the bus.

Baba Ibeji handed him some cash, and he hopped off as the bus slowed down at the next stop.

"*Egbe*," the driver said jocularly, suggesting that the tout was a novice.

Another uniform got on, this time the green and white of the road transport workers union. The driver proffered some money, but our latest antogonist was dissatisfied.

"What kind of insult is this?" he asked.

"Insult *ko*, insult *ni*," the driver retorted, sneering.

"Guy, don't make me vex. Add something now or..."

"Or what?" Baba Ibeji queried, his eyes flashing.

"Don't waste my time, abeg. You want the thing that happened last month to happen now?"

Whatever had happened the previous month must have been of sufficient gravity to motivate Baba Ibeji to stump up. The union worker hopped off. Our driver hissed and shook his head. But he still seemed of good cheer. It was with the next contingent that things started to change.

We had not gone far when two muscle-bound men in sleeveless shirts and ripped jeans boarded the bus. I could not tell who they represented, but menaces were written all over them. Without a word, one of them reached under the steering and extracted a wad of currency. He counted the money, licking the flicking finger as he went on. When he was done counting, he stuffed more than half of the notes in his pocket and returned the rest.

"*Ode buruku*," said one of the bodybuilders in denigration of the driver as they departed. The other, whose hair was in cornrows, simulated a slapping motion. I saw the pained looked on the driver's face, but he kept quiet. It was only when they were out of earshot that he muttered the reciprocal insult, "*omo ale*."

Baba Ibeji might have been simmering at this stage, but it was not obvious until another entourage accosted the bus. The traffic wardens, or "yellow fever" as they were known, again for the colour of their uniforms, were in a bad mood.

"See you, you wanted to jam us this morning, *abi*? Today, you will see pepper."

"God forbid! Me?" the incredulous driver queried. "Not me at all, at all!"

"Shut up! It is you."

Back and forth went accusation and denial until the conductor ambled up from the rear to corroborate his driver's claims that it was their first journey on the route that day. Eventually, the familiar passage of money occurred.

Transporters are supposed to be used to this sort of thing in the city, but something must have been off with Baba Ibeji that day. Maybe the twins had kept him awake all night. Whatever it was, he seemed to withdraw into a shell after the yellow fever waved us on.

On the cusp of the third mainland bridge, we came upon a roadblock mounted by men of the vehicle inspection department. Baba Ibeji slowed down late. The bus came to a screeching halt inches away from the cordon formed of old tires and hoarding.

"Bloody fool, you want to kill us, *abi*?" their leader raged. "*Oya*, bring all the papers of this bus—I want to see everything."

I could see that Baba Ibeji's hands were shaking as he gave them the papers. Other passengers in the bus were not paying attention as I was. They were more interested in the antics of a passenger peddling *otapiapia*, a magic potion of a cure for everything "from waist pain to weak organ."

By the time the vehicle inspectors released us, Baba Ibeji had been relieved of more money, despite his protestations that his papers were current and complete. When we set off again, he was no longer talking to anyone. Every now and then, he mopped his brow with one end of the towel around his neck. I tried to engage him.

"These people are a real problem, eh, *oga* driver?" I offered.

He ignored me. I noticed that his hands were trembling and there was a twitch on the side of his face.

Finally, we came upon road safety marshals in maroon shirts and black trousers. They made Baba Ibeji pull up in the service lane. "Get down," their leader ordered. "You have contravened road safety regulations." Baba Ibeji tried to argue but was met with the command, "Obey before complain!" Baba Ibeji got down.

Discussions quickly became animated. By this time, some of us in the bus were craning our necks to see what was happening. The conductor tried to intervene, and we saw the marshals motioning that he should get back onto the bus. Baba Ibeji turned on his heels as if to accompany his conductor. One of the marshals grabbed him by his trousers, and all hell broke loose.

Like I said, Baba Ibeji was slightly built. The marshals were bigger than him. Three of them surrounded him. First, he pushed hard, two-handed, on the marshal clutching his trousers so that the marshal staggered back and fell. Another marshal jumped on Baba Ibeji from behind, grabbing him by the neck and head in a choke hold. Baba Ibeji reached backwards and, bending, threw the man over in a somersault so that the man landed on the first marshal whom Baba had floored.

Baba Ibeji squared up to the third marshal and swung with his right fist. The punch missed, which was fortunate for the driver's adversary because it was the kind that kung fu movie aficionados call "one blow, seven die." However, its slipstream seemed to unbalance the marshal, for he tumbled onto the other two. Baba Ibeji was standing over them, his hands raised, and howling like a mad man. He was visibly frothing at the mouth. Suddenly, the three marshals got up and fled.

Baba Ibeji pursued them for a few yards, then slumped onto his knees and started crying. It took bystanders and some passengers from the bus, including me, over ten minutes to get him to recover his composure. It took at least the same time before he was able take charge of the bus again and we continued our journey.

The incident so intrigued me that I started researching everything from provocation to temporary insanity to self-defense. What I found went a long way in explaining why a mild-mannered man like Baba Ibeji could suddenly become a beast and how the law often excused the resulting behaviour. I decided to make it my area of specialisation once I left law school. It proved to be the tide in my affairs, which taken by storm, has brought me good fortune.

My Range Rover is pulling into Victoria Island now. We are stopped at a police checkpoint. My elderly driver winds the window down so that the policemen can see who is inside. They peer inside, see me and cheer, "Di Law, Baba Provoke. All correct, carry on, sir." My driver turns to me, beaming, and says, "Sir, they know they cannot provoke with you." I smile and reply, "Baba Ibeji, you are the true Baba Provoke." He laughs, and we continue on our way.

WHEN IT RAINED

The rain in Port Harcourt is like a long-distance runner. It is not at all muscular and explosive like the bulked-up sprinter whose exertions, for all his prancing and preening before the race, are over in seconds. No, the rain in good old "Pitakwa" is slim and sinewy, lightweight even, but, boy, does it have stamina. Once it starts, it can just keep going—pitter-patter, pitter-patter, pitter-patter—for hours on end, without tiring and, sometimes, for whole days and nights. It is weightier, admittedly, if only just, than London's similarly drudging fare but possesses nothing near the ferocity of the dark, angry and vociferous thunderstorms that ravage Abuja for no more than a bruising quarter of an hour before giving way to bright sunshine and a sweltering heat.

On the morning Iyowuna was arrested, the rain was in high season in June and running one of its marathons over Port Harcourt. Having started early Friday evening, it had plodded on through the night, dampening the spirits of aspiring revelers and causing them to retreat indoors, prematurely, to more intimate nocturnal pursuits, so that police checkpoints were thereby deprived of the elevated rate of custom that the start of the weekend usually brought. The rain continued without any sign of letting up the next morning and that, perhaps, was ultimately why Iyowuna's arrest happened.

If it had not been raining, some people would have been sitting outside, others would be going about their business, children would have been playing all over the place and Iyowuna would not have been so conspicuous. The hood of his Rockets sweatshirt would certainly not have been up over his head, and he would not have been hunched over, his hands in his pockets, looking around shiftily like one scoping the place, whereas all he wanted was somewhere dry where he could take shelter from the incessant rain.

It was later said that it was the Ikwerre landlord of the premises—a cluster of whitewashed low bungalows with rusty tin roofs situated on a dirt track off Rumuola Road—who had called the police on Iyowuna after he had been pacing up and down in the rain for about an hour. That part of the story cannot be true because, as those who know the area will readily testify, the compound was owned by a man whom everyone called a Calabar man, notwithstanding that he was actually a man from Akwa Ibom.

Others say that no one called anybody; rather, the special anti-robbery squad, or SARS for short, just happened to be passing by at the time and saw Iyowuna looking into the window of one of the low houses, which, as we shall later see, was the house rented by his brother. "Brother" is used loosely, because the tenant was just a townsman whom Iyowuna had come to visit to see if he could find Iyowuna a job at the hotel where he worked, in GRA Phase Two, near the Polo Club.

Iyowuna had stayed the course through SSCEs at Nyemoni Grammar School in Abonnema—nothing less being expected of the son of a proud, if impecunious, catechist in the Anglican Church. It was then time to try his luck in the big city and forswear, as his *isam*-seller mother hoped, life as a fisherman or a thief of crude oil in the fetid swamps of the Niger Delta.

Luck was, however, not something on Iyowuna's side the day he arrived to seek his brother's beneficence. There was no way, for instance, that the strapping, dark-complexioned, six-footer who was barely out of his teens and visiting Port Harcourt for only the third time in his life, could have known that armed robbers had visited the next compound just two nights before.

It was not raining the night the robbers conducted their operation, but there was no light. The electricity supply company said it was carrying out "load shedding," which meant it was rotating power supply between neighbourhoods. The local neighbourhood association had decreed at their meeting six months prior that when there was no power, all generators had to be "switch off at twelve o'clock sharp in the midnight" so that resident vigilantes could hear and act as appropriate when there was a disturbance in the wee hours that night marauders favoured.

Accordingly, the whole area was in darkness when the robbers knocked on the cast-iron gate of the next compound at about two o'clock in the morning. Roused from slumber by the insistent knocking, Papa Joe, the security man, croaked, "Who is that?" to which the robbers heartily replied, "We are armed robbers. Come and open this gate so that we can do and be going."

The robbers, who numbered about twenty, looked to be in their twenties and carried AK-47s, spent over an hour on the premises, going from house to house and room to room collecting money, phones, watches and whatever other valuables they could fit in the rucksacks that each of them carried. They were heard to be singing songs of praise as they went about aggregating their loot, although some of the people robbed, including Owhonda, a student-union activist who was able to decipher the voiced lyrics, claimed the songs were really cultic anthems.

SARS did not arrive until three hours later, as day was breaking, and the robbers were long gone to Amadi-Ama or whatever other Ama waterside that served as their hideout. As for the vigilantes for whom the little generators had been switched off so that they could be alerted to any unusual noises, the less said about their absence that night, the better.

It was into the aftermath of these unfortunate events that Iyowuna unknowingly ventured on the Saturday morning, having caught the first bus out of Buguma. The SARS patrol pickup had driven past the turnoff on Rumuola Road when one of the policemen remembered that there had been an incident there two nights before. The pickup screeched to a spattering halt on the wet tarmac before proceeding to reverse deliberately into the untarred side road. As it rolled past the so-called Calabar man's compound, bobbing gently up and down on the undulating track, there was a hooded Iyowuna, the only person outside in the rain, peering into the window of his brother's house.

"Halt!" ordered the patrol commander, and the driver duly obliged him. "Copul, go bring that boy here."

Two of the corporals bounded down in the rain and confronted a puzzled Iyowuna.

"See, you this boy, our *oga* want to see you."

"Why? Why does he want to see me?" Iyowuna replied, his brow creasing.

"You are asking me?" said the one who had spoken to him. "Come and ask *oga* yourself o."

Iyowuna looked from the policemen to their guns and decided it was in the interest of peace and progress to oblige. He was not afraid though. There was no reason for him to be. The two corporals, their boots squelching in the reddish-brown, waterlogged soil, shepherded him to the passenger's window of the cabin of the pickup, where the commander was seated.

"What are you finding in this place?" the commander asked, as Iyowuna bent down towards the window.

"I came to find my brother," Iyowuna replied, happy to be talking to someone rather than skulking around in the uncompromising rain.

"Who be your brother?"

"His name is Douere Ekio. He is the chief security officer at Meridian Hotel. It is like he is still at work—maybe he is on overtime."

Iyowuna announced Douere's particulars proudly. The whole clan was proud of their brother, the chief security officer. It was said back home that even the policemen assigned to guard duty at the hotel took orders from Douere, and this was the biggest hotel in Port Harcourt, where all the white people stayed when they came to do oil business at Shell. Douere reported directly to Mr. Jean-Claude, the Frenchman managing the place, who in turn was rumoured to report directly to the state governor.

"Oh-ho, CSO for Meridian," the commander said. "So why have you not call him?"

"My battery has died," replied Iyowuna.

"And what is your own name?"

"My name is Iyowuna Briggs."

There was a brief silence while the commander sized Iyowuna up. Corporal Okemini, the one who had spoken to Iyowuna, wished the commander could just stop this useless questioning and release the boy so that they could get back into the relative comforts of the tarpaulin-canopied back of the pickup. The boy seemed harmless; any policeman worth his salt could tell that and, surely, the commander with all his experience could. Okemini did not need to be a mind reader to hazard that Corporal Ebo, his colleague, was thinking along the same lines. Both of them were, therefore, equally surprised by what the commander said next.

"Okay, you will join Copul for the back of van and we will go and take you to your brother."

Iyowuna hesitated. "You say...?"

The commander smiled. "Don't worry. I know your brother well-well. We will drop you at the hotel." Iyowuna was still uncertain but, looking down at the smiling commander, he figured that this might be one of the policemen who had reported to Douere before or knew Douere as a man whom policemen reported to. Iyowuna hefted his rucksack over his shoulder and followed the duo of Okemini and Ebo into the back of the pickup, where the rest of the SARS patrol sat.

Squeezed between the policemen, Iyowuna smelt the strong odour of *kai-kai*, the gin favoured throughout the Delta which fired up the belly and made men see things with a clarity not afforded to the ordinary eye. There was another equally pervasive aroma, a tangy scent, which if Iyowuna were more worldly wise, he would have known was the smell of unadulterated weed that the policemen bought in Amadi-Ama from the same people who sold to armed robbers and to university students like Owhonda.

As the pickup made its way into town in the rain, splashing water occasionally as it whizzed through pools collecting by the side of the road, Iyowuna relaxed. The policemen, though red-eyed to a man, were not rude to him or at all abrasive. Instead, they shared some *bole* and fish—a staple of riverine communities—with him.

Iyowuna expressed gratitude, thankful to eat his first meal of the day, delighted that it was food he was conversant with and happy to be in the company of these friendly policemen. Now, at last, he understood the jingle, "Police is Your Friend," that often played on radio. But he wondered even more why his mother always hissed when the song came on.

Iyowuna would not have been so elated had he known that if the policemen were indeed taking him to the Meridian, they would have turned right at the junction at which they stopped to buy the *bole* and fish, by the imposing Manuchim Chambers. Instead, the pickup continued along Aba Road, heading deeper into the bowels of a sodden metropolis, towards Old Port Harcourt Township.

Police stations have a peculiar smell, and it is not a good smell. There are many reasons for this. The sheer volume of human traffic in and out of the station brings with it all sorts of odours, especially given the unyielding tropical heat and the fact that many of the patrons belong to a demographic for which toothpaste, perfumes and deodorants are unaffordable or unknown unguents. However, the major contributor to the smell that cloaks the police station, to the point of asphyxiation if a strong draft blows through the premises, is the cell.

All the commingling odours in the station are magnified in the invariably overcrowded police cell. This, of course, is only to be expected when men who are packed like sardines into an enclosed space are not privileged to have washed in many days and, to make matters worse, have only a bucket in the corner to relieve themselves in. The cell, for those unfortunate to make its acquaintance, provides a foretaste of that place of torment with which it rhymes and in which *Ekwensu* is rumored to live.

It was into such a theatre of deprivation that Iyowuna was thrown into, at the Old Cemetery Police Station. Iyowuna did not suspect anything when the patrol pickup pulled into the station. He assumed that the policemen wanted to change vehicles or drop some of them off. Then they told him to get down, and he thought that perhaps the commander had called Douere to meet them here.

Iyowuna only started to have the feeling that something strange was afoot when he got inside the station. There was no sign of Douere.

He was asked to step behind the counter even as he shook off the rain, and, while it was a politely framed request, an alarm went off inside his head. One of the policemen at the counter asked his name and age and wrote inside a register as he answered. The alarm bells rang louder when the SARS policeman that had brought him in took aside the policeman with the register and they started talking in low tones, looking over their shoulders from time to time at him.

Iyowuna thought about making a break for it. The entrance into the station had no door and he could see outside, through the continuing rain to the main road, past where the patrol commander was now reaching out of the pickup to scribble in the register held open under an umbrella by a stooping policeman from the counter. The station was, however, a beehive of policemen, and he did not think he would get far. Where did he even think he was and where would he go? Besides, he had not done anything, and running might make it seem like he had. Yet the klaxon in his head was now going off at full blast.

The patrol pickup screeched off shortly after, and the policeman with the register came back into the building. He was no longer smiling.

"Take off your clothes," he barked at the young man as he set the register on the counter.

"You say…?" Iyowuna asked tentatively.

"My friend, I don't have time to argue with armed robber. I say remove your shirt, trouser and shoe now, now."

Armed robber? Had the policeman just called him an armed robber? "See officer—" Iyowuna started, taking a step forwards so that he was squaring up to the policeman.

The slap was a regulation police slap: sudden, aimed across the cheek and eye, and struck, palm flayed wide, with the utmost force. The sound of its contact resonated through the station. Iyowuna was nearly knocked to the ground. Staggering backwards, he put his hands on the wall to steady himself, a constellation of stars circulating in his immediate line of vision. He touched the side of his face where the slap had landed as if to check that his face was intact.

Rage exploded inside him, and he made for the man who had slapped him, but the police are used to this kind of thing and, as if by magic, there were suddenly three or four other policemen —to Iyowuna they felt like a dozen—grabbing his hands behind his back and pushing him face first against the wall. The policeman who'd slapped him grabbed a baton from under the counter and started swinging it at Iyowuna's calves and the backs of his knees. Iyowuna felt his legs give way under the force and pain of the blows.

To cut a short story shorter, the policemen forcibly stripped him to his underpants before carrying him, horizontally between them at waist level, down the corridor that ran the length of one side of the station towards the cell that was the corridor's terminus. The baton kept swinging across the back of his torso during the short journey to the iron-grilled door which served as the entrance to the cell and its only source of ventilation and lighting.

There is a hierarchy in police cells that loosely mimics—in subversion and mockery but also out of necessity—the chain of command under whose auspices the confinement exists, so that the cell Iyowuna was thrown into had, as is customary, a commander, a second in command ("Two-I-C") and an aide-de-camp ("ADC") exercising authority over lesser ranking inmates. Iyowuna was not to know all this until he was plunged into the sea of unwashed bodies. He found himself savagely pushed and pummeled until he was huddled next to the bucket in the far reaches of the cell.

Bruised and battered, Iyowuna was in a daze. As a figure jostled through the throng to stand over him, he put his hands over his head, expecting the worst.

"I am the Two-I-C in this barracks," the man in tattered Y-Fronts announced. "C'mon get up—you must be upstanding when speaking to superior officer."

Iyowuna looked up and around. He was the center of attention of a mass of dark-circled eyes and haggard, unshaven faces. He was completely disoriented, but from somewhere inside the fog of his confusion and bewilderment, he mustered the will to focus. Iyowuna tried to stand but discovered his legs were still acting of their own accord after the disjunction that the baton caused. Despite his best efforts, he wobbled back down, dropping onto his buttocks and only narrowly avoiding slamming his hand into the bucket as he tried to arrest his fall. His predicament brought mirth to Two-I-C and some of the nearest men, who burst into laughter.

"See, Two-I-C, that is enough." It was a grave voice from the other end of the room. Even in his distress, Iyowuna realised that the laughter stopped immediately.

"Yes, sah!" Two-I-C stamped one foot next to the other, saluted sharply and wheeled round towards the voice, jostling his way back as he had come.

"See, everybody move, I want to see that boy again." The baritone voice from the end of the cell came once again with authority.

The inmates leaned apart in tandem to open a clear line of vision from one end of the cell to the other. Iyowuna looked up, through the corridor created in the sea of near-naked bodies, towards the voice. It belonged to a bearded man whose muscular physique took Iyowuna's mind immediately to the thugs who'd invaded Kalabari land on Election Day, shooting up and down, and hijacking ballot boxes.

The bearded man was sitting down against the wall at the far corner of the cell and was in the luxury of such space, in contrast to all the other inmates, that his legs were stretched out freely and fully. He was wearing jean shorts which, though tattered and filthy, differentiated him from the other prisoners who, as far as Iyowuna could see, wore only underpants. One of the underwear-clad was fanning the big man with the kind of raffia fan that *bole* sellers use to fan their charcoal braziers.

"ADC, go help Two-I-C bring that armed robber here to Commander."

"Yes sah, Commander, sah," ADC said, putting down the fan.

ADC loped over the bodies of the huddled inmates until he was standing over Iyowuna. He and Two-I-C put their hands under Iyowuna's armpits and dragged him backwards across the cell, bumping into and stumbling over some of the huddled prisoners who swore angrily but did not offer more. The two aides propped Iyowuna into a sitting position by the wall beside Commander. Oblivious to their grumbling, Commander ordered the inmates closest to him to move to yield space.

"You want water?" Commander asked, proffering a sachet of water which seemed to have materialised from nowhere. Iyowuna declined with a shake of his head and Commander shook his in return as if to say, "You don't know where you are yet." Commander drank all the water, his giant Adam's apple bobbing, before motioning to ADC to resume the fanning. They sat in silence like that for a long time, the only sounds from within the cell being the swish-swish of the fan and the coughing of the inmates. Above and beyond them, the rain continued, rat-a-tat-a-tat, on the zinc roof of the station.

"Why did you call me armed robber?" Iyowuna had recovered enough of his composure to speak up.

ADC looked sharply at him and then to Commander, as if to seek directions on how to punish this petulance, but Commander motioned to ADC to continue fanning.

"You be armed robber o," Commander said, almost wearily, without looking at Iyowuna. "It is only armed robber that police can beat like that."

Iyowuna began to frame a protest, but Commander made one of the hand gestures that Iyowuna now understood to mean that he should keep quiet.

They sat in silence some more. Morning had become afternoon and still the rain showed no sign of abating. Iyowuna's mind raced furiously. Armed robber? He had never robbed anybody in his life. The policemen in the pickup had not accused him of anything. Their friendliness only heightened his confusion. Surely, the desk sergeant had made a mistake? "Commander, sir," he whispered, adopting the protocol he now recognised to prevail in the cell, "permission to speak, sir?"

"What now?" Commander grunted, though smiling at this quick learner. The boy did not seem like a hard man, much less an armed robber, but you could never tell these days with all these boys who watched American rappers doing *gangsta* on TV and thought they too could do *gangsta* in real life.

"Commander, don't be annoyed, but I am not an armed robber," Iyowuna said. "I just came to see my brother Douere Ekio, the CSO of—"

"Meridian Hotel?" Commander completed, perking up. "Senior Douere is your brother?"

"Yes, yes," Iyowuna whispered quickly, a wave of relief washing over him that Commander knew Douere.

"Aha, small world. Douere used four classes to senior me at Nyemoni Grammar School. He is a good man. I see him when we follow candidate to go lodge at the hotel during last elections. But how comes you enter inside this bad place?"

Iyowuna proceeded to narrate the events of the morning. Commander listened with a frown, never taking his eyes off Iyowuna's face as the young man spoke. When Iyowuna finished, Commander nodded several times, stroking his beard, his expression pensive.

"Can you help me, Commander, abeg?" Iyowuna implored, his voice still barely a whisper.

"Not now, maybe in the night. But you must to stay this side," Commander said, his voice suddenly lower than even Iyowuna's. "We shall see in the night."

"In the night—?"

"Enough talking!" Commander suddenly raised his voice, cutting off Iyowuna. "No more talking for now—I want to rest."

Startled, Iyowuna fell silent, but he was grateful he could stay by Commander's side where there was at least a bit of space to stretch one leg from time to time. He could still smell the stench from the bucket from this end of the cell and marveled at his luck for Commander to know Douere. Only God knew how he would have coped beside that bucket.

The rain continued as evening gave way to night. A faint glow, the residue of light from the naked bulbs in the rest of the station, provided the only semblance of illumination in the windowless cell which grew ever dimmer as the station wound down for the night. Eventually the last light, the one over the counter, also went off, although the inmates could never be sure whether that was voluntary or the Port Harcourt electricity supply company had struck. Nobody, not even the police, was immune from a bit of load shedding.

Sleep crept into the cell like a practiced thief and began stealing the prisoners' consciousness one by one. Iyowuna was determined not to succumb, but the weight of exhaustion from an unfathomable day had other ideas. The rain had at last begun to wane, but its diminished drumbeat became the sweet lullaby assailing his last bastion of resistance.

He pulled up his knees to his chest, wrapping his arms around them, and turned his head towards the ceiling. He did not know how long he had been staring upwards when green smoke started coming from the ceiling. He glanced around desperately, but all the inmates were fast asleep. He tried to stand but could not feel his lower body. The smoke thickened and started to obscure his vision.

Suddenly, a face emerged from the smoke. It was Commander's, but quickly became the patrol commander's face. Then it was Douere's, and his mother's, and then his father's. Their lips were moving. He could not make out anything at first but soon realised they were calling his name. He tried desperately to answer, but the smoke was now in his mouth, choking him. He woke with a start.

There was a small beam of light in the cell, directed towards where the bucket was. He was relieved he had only been dreaming, but there was still a vice-like grip over his mouth. He looked sideways to Commander and, even in the gloom, could see the bearded man wag a finger. And then Commander took his hand off Iyowuna's mouth and rolled away.

Iyowuna heard his name again. This was not his father but an unfamiliar voice at the cell door, just over the source of the light.

"Iyowuna Briggs. This is your last chance. Your people have come to bail you—come out now."

Iyowuna's eyes were better adjusted to the darkness, and he realised there were figures outside the cell door. One of them was holding the torch whose beam raked the cell. As the light passed by him and Commander, Commander spoke up.

"Officer, please now, it is like maybe they have released that one. Abeg, let us sleep in this our barracks now."

The beam held steady on Commander for a moment and then zigzagged across the cell again.

"Iyowuna Briggs."

Fully alert now, Iyowuna stifled the urge to answer.

"Let us go." It was the voice that had called his name. "It is like they have released that one, true-true."

"All these useless desk-sergeant people," another of the figures outside hissed. "They just like to waste person's time for nothing."

The beam was cut, and the shadowy figures retreated from the cell door. Shortly thereafter, the sound of a vehicle driving off from the station could be heard.

Iyowuna realised he was bathed in sweat and his heart beat painfully in his chest. Still, he was confused as to what had happened, and a part of him wondered whether he should have spoken up. The answer was not long forthcoming.

About ten minutes after the visitors had departed, a shout pierced the night. It seemed to come from behind the wall of the cell but, in truth, was from the nearby cemetery from which the station derived its name. The cry was followed by a string of small explosions that sounded to Iyowuna like "knockout," the firecrackers he let off with his friends on New Year's Eve. But who was throwing knockout at this time of the year? There was a slight pause, and then he heard the shout again—it was clearer now that Iyowuna was straining his ears, and it appeared to be an order. Again, a volley of crackling sounds, reminiscent of knockout, followed. Then there was silence.

Commander nudged Iyowuna and grunted.

"Those people that call your name—every weekend they just come in the midnight and gather all the suspected armed robbers in all the stations in the town and carry them to Old Cemetery. There, firing squad, ta-ta-ta-ta, no wasting time. Had it been that you answered them, your own for done finish by now."

A little after seven o'clock the next morning, Douere Ekio strode into the Old Cemetery Police Station with a friend of his, an assistant superintendent of police and one of the policemen who worked with him to provide security at the hotel. It had been a frantic inquiry after a neighbour alerted Douere of "one boy like that" whom the SARS patrol had picked up outside his bungalow.

The two men stomped past the counter to the Divisional Police Officer's office which, in typical police irony, was situated next to the malodourous cell, notwithstanding that it was the ranking office in the station. Shortly thereafter, the desk sergeant, the same one who knew how to slap, hurried into the DPO's office, clutching the register with frayed edges.

"He has been released, sir," the desk sergeant said, opening the register to show where Iyowuna Briggs' release was recorded.

"Nonsense!" Douere exclaimed, standing up and striding out to the door of the cell. Holding on to the iron bars he called out, "Iyowuna, brother is here—are you there?"

This time, Iyowuna knew to answer.

HEADSTRONG

If I tell you now that I choked on my burger, you will say that these *ajebutter* people have come again. But if it were you, *nko?* Sitting across from your madam, you see the name of your side chick in print— would that one alone not make you fear? Then you see what she has written about. Chai. That she had an affair with this big man. Oh my God. This is in *The New Yorker.* Can you imagine? Not one nonsense blog or all these *tatafo* sites that serious people don't read. *The New Yorker.* The devil is a liar!

Eka and I had just finished the Degas retrospective at the Houston Museum of Fine Arts. You don't know Degas? Forget o. Bad man Impressionist. You don't know that one, too? Sorry, that's how I roll with wifey. Strictly bougie, hashtag *oyibo* moves.

She was on the phone, regaling her sister. We had googled the artist before we went. You should have seen us flex as our new knowledge came alive in the exhibition. Of course, we were the only black people there, a usual something, but it must be mentioned.

My sister-in-law lived in New York, which made me remember the magazine subscription I hardly used. That was how I carried my own hand and decided to browse the latest edition. And that was how my double cheeseburger suddenly started choking me.

"Are you alright, honey?" Eka asked, hand over phone, wide-eyed.

"*Kpohor, kpohor,*" was all I could manage. So, waving my assurances, I made for the restroom and locked myself in a cubicle. Guy, my heart was just beating anyhow in my chest as I started to skim that story.

She called it "Birdsong." Those birds clearly made as much of an impression on her as I had. The fruit trees attracted them to the compound on Victoria Island. After sex, we would lounge in the verandah on the first floor, barely dressed, watching the birds frolic. Naturally, their chirping became a soundtrack of sorts to the torrid affair she chronicled.

And chronicle she did, in detail. Celcom's head office where I first saw the *mami wata.* Our love nest, the charming colonial guesthouse. The discrete restaurant in Ikoyi that I always took her to. Emma, my driver, whom she had problems with from day one. Chichi, her best friend at work, who empathised with my girl's constant rebellions but conformed herself anyway.

And me? See searching for my name. It wasn't a small thing. She confessed to struggling with calling a middle-aged man of means her "boyfriend." Instead, he was her "lover," the one who always took off his wedding ring before coitus and meticulously deleted her messages from his phone.

Make no mistake, she left clues left, right and center about this lover's identity. But she did not drop a name. That was very important. I serve a living God, my bro. My mood started to lift like *ijebu-garri*.

There are thousands of big boys in Lagos who might fit the description. Even my guy, one of the *awon-boyz* who shared my haunts and pastimes, could be the courtly, bespectacled, dark-as-Gambian sugar daddy she described. That this man had a scar above the navel was neither here nor there—am I the only one with that kind of mark?

And then I saw it. The lover, she wrote, signed off phone messages with "CWAD." Cock with a dick. Chai. That girl has killed me finally. If I like, let me talk from now until tomorrow, but this one I could not deny, especially not to Eka. Something that started as a little joke is what wants to send me to an early grave now.

There were two birds mating that day on the guava tree. Kingfishers, she wrote, but frankly, I don't remember; how do women memorialise little details like that? I recall, however, that we had just finished what the birds were doing. I was thinking about how like birds we were—hadn't Scripture even asked us to learn from them and stop worrying?—when a remarkable difference occurred to me.

"Do you know that most birds don't have penises?"

"What? Are you serious?"

It always felt good to educate her.

"Yes o," I replied, smiling. "All beak, no dick."

She pondered my revelation for a moment. In a town like this, where sycophancy is the number one virtue, and *oga*—be he sugar daddy, husband or boss—is never wrong, even when chatting dust, my girl was a breath of fresh air. It was one of the many things that made me love her die.

"No now, you can't deceive me like that," she said. "My mother had poultry when I was a child—I used to see them mate."

"To mate is one thing," I countered, "but have you ever seen a cock with a dick?"

She laughed even before I caught it. My mistress was quick—another thing I loved.

"Too funny, baby, too funny," she said, wagging a finger. "Come here, you naughty boy."

My next message to her ended "C with a D." She replied with a string of love emojis, and CWAD became my signature sign-off.

Look at the big deal she's made of it in *The New Yorker*, using big English like "symbolisms of trust," "zones of exclusivity" and so on. Ma-ami, it was just a joke now? Abeg now? Please, what is this thing of women always hunting for deeper meaning in what people say to them? Even, my mistress, my stubborn nonconformist?

"What's wrong, baby?" Eka's question jolted me.

"Wh-why, darling?" I stammered.

"Because you're not saying anything now," she said, smiling sweetly. "And see, frowning!"

We were already in Sugarland but honestly, if you ask me how we got there, my best answer would be "by His mercy." Don't laugh. I had navigated traffic, turned right and left, sped up and slowed down, entered the highway and exited, but not once had my mind been on the road or what I was doing. My forced normalcy upon returning to Eka in the café had since lapsed into a stony silence as all my mind went to that article.

I can only thank God that wifey decided not to go shopping in the Galleria after all. "Let's spend the rest of the day at home, baby" she suggested instead. "It's not every weekend I get to see my big C with a D."

What? Wait, don't be looking at me with that kind of shocked expression. Hear me out first.

Yes, I began to use "CWAD" on messages to Eka as well, having found a way to sneak the joke into conversation with her. And, no, it wasn't a mistake at all. I messaged her all the time in between chatting with my girl. Sometimes, I even copied and pasted to one a nice message sent to the other. So I didn't want Eka to see a strange signature one day—women have a way of picking up on such innocuous slips.

That guyman plan had, unfortunately, manufactured the time-bomb on my hands. Eka had a subscription to *The New Yorker*. It was only a matter of time before her woman radar *jejely* went to that story.

The affair was a by-product of my doing the state governor's bidding. We were having a solid lunch at Government House—*efo riro*, *amala* and things—scheming this and that as usual, when the rambunctious Oba stormed in. He had no time for pleasantries: "*Oti o*, if it is trouble that these Celcom people want, I will show them pepper o."

Me, I was just admiring the deep tribal marks twitching like embedded whiskers on Oba's face as he let off a string of curses. The tirade ended with an invocation of ancestral spirits residing in the lagoon to act against the company. As royal fathers cannot be seen eating in public, Kabiyesi declined the governor's perfunctory invitation to join us at the table and left as dramatically as he came.

His Excellency was obliged to help. Even a small child knows that he would never have been governor but for thousands of pre-marked ballots that miraculously appeared from Oba's palace in the evening of Election Day. I went to Celcom from Government House, hoping to arrive ahead of vengeful figures from the lagoon.

Anyone that the governor's chief of staff had called ahead of was no ordinary emissary and the general manager, Mr. Abiodun, knew that. Come and see bowing. His grip was firm but sweaty as he led me across the open-plan office towards his table. It was "sir, this" and "sir, that" as he sought to ingratiate himself with the clear and present receptacle of power before him. I wasn't paying attention.

Because, come and see babe. *Warada*! Low-cut hair, minimal makeup, but see natural beauty. Her face was chiseled like a statue's and, I swear, no bleaching cream had ever tainted that dark-chocolate skin. I placed her…late twenties. Even on first sight, rebellion was writ large on her face.

"So, sir, how is the family, sir?"

I barely heard the question through the fog of my fascination with the mirage to my left, but as a sharp man, I seized on it. We were nearly abreast of her table. Raising my voice, I answered.

"The family is fine. They're in America."

Small words, but gigantic statement. You trust now. Money, status, eligibility. My family is in America. Powerful. A mating call like no other in this Lagos.

She would later tell me, and repeat in *The New Yorker*, that I said it in an "Americanah" accent, the sort that is switched on to impress people but disappears as soon as the purveyor loses his or her cool. If you ever read the story, pay no heed to her mocking tone. Because that day, from the corner of my eyes, I saw her perk up. True, she sneered, but a little too overtly, and she held her gaze.

The meeting with Mr. Abiodun was briefer than it should have been. He was garbling assurances—"I cannot disobey my governor, sir; I am so happy to meet you, sir"—when I brought out my business card and a really expensive pen. On my way out, I passed by her table and, meeting her eyes, carefully placed the card before her. On the back I had scrawled, "Wow is an understatement."

The next day, I had Emma deliver a hardcover edition of *We Should All Be Feminists*, nicely wrapped, along with a large bouquet, to Celcom. I received a message on my phone: "Thanks. Love it. Wow is not overstatement. LOL."

With many other young women in Lagos, I would have been better served by putting a thousand dollars in an envelope. Not this rebel. I read and reread the text before deleting it.

We went to the fine-dining restaurant in Ikoyi owned by my chubby and gregarious friend, Philip, whose grandparents had migrated from Lebanon in the 1960s. With neither signboard nor website, Philip's was known only to select clientele. Senior boys like me could entertain there, in the dim interior, without fear of running into someone we should not run into.

She did not object to my suggestion that we retire to the guest-house in Victoria Island. I told her it belonged to Philip but that I was borrowing it while my house was being renovated. As I showed her around, her eyes narrowed.

"This doesn't belong to Philip, does it? It's yours, isn't it?"

I mumbled incomprehensibly but that did the trick.

She giggled. "Sweet," she said, kissing me on the cheek. "Modesty is so sexy." As she strode onto the verandah to admire the view, I permitted myself a broad grin. The little girl. The house was one of His Excellency's.

"Our friend, the governor," Eka announced, a nod to the Timaya "Money" ringtone. We were looking at the flamingos on our lawn when the phone rang. I chatted briefly with His Excellency, laughing when he said the Oba called me a "magic-shan," then passed him on to Eka. From her giggling, I made out he was telling her not to break my waist or something like that. Ah, His Excellency, my friend, my benefactor.

I do things for the governor I cannot tell you. No, don't be silly. Nothing like *juju* and blood rituals. This is not Nollywood. Let us just say that I am his trustee, managing confidential assets. To make sure he is very okay when he leaves office. And that Kuje Prison shall never be his portion.

My mistress, of course, did not know what I did. She confessed in print to being curious, like many a kept woman, but unable to explain what stopped her from inquiring. "These governors won't let somebody rest," was the most I offered, after taking another call out of earshot. Her own was to grimace, but the empowered gleam in her eyes told everything.

Sometimes, of course, it was not a politician on the line but the most powerful person in my life—my Eka dearest. I never spoke about Eka or the children. But I let my mistress know she had no hope of displacing them. The first time we made love, I laid down the marker.

"When you want to settle down, I won't stand in your way." My tone was buoyant. "I'm not like all these selfish married men who want to have their cake and eat it."

If a pin had dropped in the silence that followed, you would have heard it.

"That's...very...considerate," she eventually said and curled up with her back to me.

That wasn't the kind of reaction I expected at all, knowing how she carried on normally. But I didn't dwell on it, especially because, as she recounted in *The New Yorker,* we then proceeded to date for "thirteen months and eight days," during which she did everything possible to poke her finger in the eye of society.

My laughing wasn't small at the consternation her Marlboro habit caused workmates who considered that only prostitutes smoked in public. She was the sole and unyielding objector, a vocal one at that, to the prayer meetings Mr. Abiodun held every Monday in the office. "You should *comot* o," Kehinde, the secretary, and a prayer warrior at Redemption Ministries, would say, "before one day, the thunder looking for you will now come and strike us."

Her schoolboy hair was another badge of revolt. She had little sympathy for Chichi whose thick weave caused her scalp to itch but prevented her fingers from getting through. "See me, see trouble," my mistress giggled, mimicking the way Chichi slapped her head continually to assuage the itch. I never mentioned of course that Chichi had once slipped me her number when my mistress wasn't looking, but that is another story.

My mistress preferred documentaries to soaps. We discussed stories from *Business Day* and *Bloomberg* and oohed and aahed over the similarity of our views. She genuinely liked sports; not for her was the Lagos girls' act of putting up with SuperSport but switching to Africa

Magic as soon as the man left the room. I remember the day I teased her about supporting Chelsea—ol' boy, she stunned me by coolly recounting, in between Marlboros, the club's perennial lows before Russian money arrived. "God, you're so different!" was all I could muster, and not for the first time.

"Here, baby, you can catch up on the first season while I rustle up something." Eka was handing me the remote for some comedy whose characters did song and dance to vent their innermost feelings. "You'll see yourself in them, you and your always trying to sing, baby," she laughed into the kitchen. I slumped on the sofa, trying in vain to concentrate on the blur of images on the screen.

My wife had only a passing interest in serious TV. The nine to five, or seven more like, of an epidemiology professor at Houston Genetics was suffused with enough seriousness to last many lifetimes. Home for her was a sanctuary of rest and relaxation, a place for love, laughter and the unabashedly facetious, like keeping up with Kim K.

While I watched my football at weekends, she did Pilates by the pool or went shopping. We attended exhibitions and the exclusive charity galas that appeared in *Houston Modern Luxury*. Dining out otherwise was reserved for birthdays and anniversaries; Eka could not bear Texas-sized portions—"I can't come and be fat for my C with a D o"—but she could whip up a storm with a few lentils, the aroma now wafting from our really expensive kitchen confirming so.

My mistress cook? *Taa*. I wasn't even sure she could boil an egg. But I enjoyed having her around so much that I didn't complain when, little by little, her dresses and creams began to fill the bedroom shelves in the guesthouse. At least it meant she did not have to drive back late to the tiny flat in Ikate which always worried me—my brother, between armed robbers and SARS police checkpoints, the *wahala* in this Lagos is too much.

Rebel *si*, rebel *asiro*, she loved presents and I gave plenty—a Rolex for her birthday, De Beers bracelet on Valentine's, LV here, Gucci there. As a large boy is concerned. Yet, the first time I tried to give money, she accused me of treating her like a prostitute: "So I'm now the *akwuna*, eh?" she queried, ignoring the wad of notes in my hand. This my girl and her forming. I knew she could do with money.

Her car told the story. A used—*Tokunbo*—Corolla, probably imported through Cotonou by dealers who did anyhow with odometers, it bore scar upon scar of the daily warfare that is Lagos traffic. Anytime my peacock pulled up, "Beauty and the Beast" would start playing in my head.

So I started leaving envelopes of cash on the kitchen table, marked "for petrol" or "for lunch." As if she could eat two hundred dollars' worth of meat pie. The envelopes were gone when I came back from work. We never talked about them, but she would hug me and whisper, "Thank you, my generous C widda D."

Our evenings were spent in the guesthouse or dawdling over lobster and plantains at Philip's. She was into no-holds-barred sex, like me, so we made love often and fiercely. She confided how much she resented her parents for making her feel an unworthy replacement for the son they never had. I lied about my father's penury in retirement being my driving force. She said blue suited me best, chose my outfits accordingly, and cooed with pleasure at seeing them on me in the weekend paper pull-outs, often beside His Excellency.

And then, bam, just like that, she wanted more.

There was this band playing at the Thistle Bar we should see. AY at the Landmark Center would be great fun. What about Valentine's dinner at the RSVP for a change?

I was never anything but on the down-low with affairs, unlike many shameless men around here suffering acute DRS—Delayed Rocking-Life Syndrome. I loved and respected my wife too much for that, no jokes. My work also demanded comportment and discretion. So I did not drink anyhow and never smoked. And you would not catch me dead at any of those parties in Banana Island where Unilag girls in "naked cloth" were given one hundred dollars each and paired off with potbellied old men.

But the more I rebuffed my mistress, the more petulant she became. One day, she called me a bastard.

Our butterfly effect, the flapping of little wings that caused a hurricane, arrived in the form of a snack. "I'm so craving meat pies," she said, her period imminent. And not just any meat pies but from a particular patisserie on Kofo Abayomi. Emma refused her entreaties to let the Bentley idle in front of the shop while she went about her business, for fear—as he later explained to me—of being clamped by LASTMA. She stormed back in an Uber, hysterical, and not even my promise of having a word with the driver would calm her down.

Next thing: "I don't blame him; it's you. It's because of all the other girls you bring here."

I could not quite make the connection but felt no need for escalation. So I patiently explained that no, I hadn't brought any others here, and yes, I'd had one or two affairs before, but see, they weren't just any women—they were special, like her, strong women.

"You're just a bloody bastard."

"What?"

She repeated it. Slowly.

She would write that I ordered her to leave. My recollection is of saying she'd lost her mind. I sat out in the verandah while she packed and until the front door shut. I went to the bathroom. A lot of her makeup was still there. I smiled and dialed Eka.

Eka's seafood stew was the business, as usual. The right amount of spicy, it lifted my spirits. I begged that we chillax by the pool "to digest." It was a nice spring day and not yet blistering as H-town can get. Eka was game and changed into a barely-there bikini. I watched with admiration from the lounger as she made a ponytail of her lush extensions before tucking them into a swimming cap and plunging gracefully into the pool.

She counted aloud as she reached my end on each lap, "CWAD one, CWAD two..." and so on. It came out as "see wad," my wife's extension of the joke, alluding to my penchant for carrying bundles of cash in Lagos. She looked a dream in the water, my baby, full of laughter and mischief as always. I loved my wife.

I threw myself into work in the days after my mistress left the compound, including arranging an offshore trust for a Northern governor. After EFCC impounded millions of dollars from his cousin, a former minister, he "started having palpitations" and contacted His Excellency.

That weekend, reading newspapers alone on the verandah for the first time in a while, I saw that my new client's relative had gone to court claiming the seized money was "gifts from friends and well-wishers." This was the kind of story we would have laughed at together, my mistress and me. I imagined her saying, "As if it is beans..." with the tinge of sarcasm that was her trademark. I called her. She answered on the second ring, to me singing Bob Marley, "Three Little Birds."

A few days later, we had settled to where we could talk about it. I had wounded her deeply, she said, and didn't I know there were things that just shouldn't be said to a woman, and especially to her?

"So why didn't you cry then, instead of insulting me?" I teased.

"I should cry? Because your wife cries?" she shot back, her eyes on fire.

We were together again but we never went back to how we used to be. Until today, I really cannot say why my free spirit had suddenly become so sullen. Her *New Yorker* retelling accused me of being narcissistic and willfully blind to whatever it was that troubled her, but what was that now?

Was it me that told her to start entertaining notions of "possibility"—as she revealed in her story—and longing for one of the birds to swoop away with my wedding ring forever? Just look at this girl. Didn't you know I was happily married before you came and started catching cruise, doing OPP with me? And why in heaven's name would you start comparing yourself to my wife?

The driver was rude to her, she wrote, because he knew my wife—he knew he could not be reprimanded. The naivete. Which driver doesn't know both his *oga*'s madam and girlfriends? When has that ever stopped us from scolding them?

Emma was simply surly by nature, as people in his position usually are. A man who had two wives and who had just informed me proudly that he was taking a third, a twenty-year-old only five years older than his last child, had no problem with my mistress being my mistress.

The problem was my mistress. If only her constant fight-fight with convention did not blind her so much to the graces and little favours that got people by in our society. All she had to do was to dash Emma a few thousand naira every now and then. She would have been amazed at how quickly his frostiness turned to ingratiation.

I logged two weeks in Houston for Eka's birthday. Northern governor's PA called me while I was there. His *oga* was so happy with my arrangee work that as a bonus, he was gifting me a new—tear-rubber—bullet-proof Innoson SUV. How should they register it? I gave the name of my mistress.

On the eve of her birthday, Eka organised a girls' night out to La Bare. I took the opportunity to see the Houston Symphony at Jones Hall. With the orchestra killing it, I sent a message to my mistress.

"@Concert. Great Music. Calling u on speaker so u hear. CWAD."
Her number rang several times; each time she sent it to voicemail.

She was waiting for me in the guesthouse on my return to Lagos. I couldn't stop touching her hair—I'd missed it, and her, a lot. We were going to Philip's as soon as I freshened up.

I should have known once out of the bathroom that this girl had gone through my phone but by then, strong face had become such a constant with her that I didn't call it anything. She confessed in *The New Yorker* to have been crushed beyond compare to discover, in the middle of my poor rendition of "Endless Love" from the shower, that even "CWAD" was not hers alone.

In the car, she asked why I'd called her from a concert with my wife.

"Ah-ah, that was me now trying to show you how much you mean to me." It didn't hurt of course to omit that Eka hadn't been there.

"That is such bullsh—"

"Forget it, baby," I interjected. "History now."

Things didn't get better at Philip's. She lashed out at the waiter. The poor man looked at me, mortified. I asked him to give us a few minutes.

"What is wrong with you?"

She was livid. Why did he not look at her? Why did all the waiters, all the drivers, and all the messengers and gatemen in this Lagos not greet her or acknowledge her?

"Has it struck you," I said, as coolly as I could, "that maybe that is their own good manners?"

"What does that mean?"

"It means that they see you as…" I struggled for the right words, "…a queen?"

"What?" For the first time since she started the rant, she seemed a bit uncertain.

"So, do you talk to a queen anyhow? When somebody like this waiter, like Emma, sees us together they are respecting me, and you, by not talking directly to you."

"That's rubbish," she said, downing the entire glass of wine. "They should all be feminists, really."

"Ah, so that's what this is about?" I grinned. "You're still reading that book?"

"But Adichie's right, isn't she?"

"Honestly? I don't think so. This is not 'the abroad,' as you and Chichi say, you know. Here, it is when they talk to you anyhow that you should really be worried. That is when, inside them, they have no respect for you."

She started to say something, but I held up a hand. The plan had been to present the keys after dinner, but perhaps doing it now would rescue our evening.

"Guess who is the owner of a brand new, tear rubber?" I beamed.

She said nothing, her expression vacant.

"Did you hear me at all?

"I heard you alright," she snapped. "You bought me a car."

"And...?"

"So I should start jumping up and down for you now, *abi*?"

She proceeded with a monologue—something incoherent about patterns of trust and distrust in Lagos. I sat back in silence, looking at this melodramatic stranger on the fringes of insanity. Then she burst into tears. My strong woman had never cried with me before.

During the week, I flew to Abuja to meet with the governor who bought me the vehicle. When I got back, wearing a sumptuous *babanriga* befitting of one who had gone up North, the guesthouse felt cold and empty, the birds silent as if composing a dirge. The nightstand was shorn of her things. I didn't even bother checking the wardrobe. I was sad but relieved.

Eka tapped me on the shoulder, and I nearly had a heart attack. She was toweling herself and shaking her long hair, now free of her swimming cap. How long had she been there?

"Come o, see wad'm, this one that you're still reading *New Yorker,* it must be a good story—you will give me the gist later, *abi*?"

"Err…no… I mean, yes. Of course, baby."

She gave me a quizzical look. "Are you sure you're okay, baby? You haven't been the same since that burger."

"No, I'm fine." I tried to sound casual. "What about your own subscription?"

"Ah, that one? I canceled it o. We're duplicating too much. The only ones I'm keeping are the ones you don't have, like *Essence.* So you show me yours and I'll show you mine. Deal?" She brought her hand towards me for a high five.

"Of course, dear, deal." I smiled, slapping her open palm. Reprieve. For now.

EYE FOR A TOOTH

Alhaji Sani was seething, but you would not have known by looking at him. To everyone in the room, the urbane sixty-something-year-old was a picture of dignified tranquility. He was even humming under his breath which made appearances more deceptive.

Alhaji knew he had to control his temper.

"Hypertension is a silent killer," Doctor Selwyn had said. Doctor Ahmed had nodded sagely in agreement before adding, "And it is not to be joked with."

Both doctors then beamed over their Samsung tablets, in the spotless consulting suite at the spanking Châteaux Monieux Clinic on the pristine shores of Lake Geneva.

"Selah!" Alhaji responded, his eyes twinkling.

The bespoke-suited doctors permitted themselves a chuckle, again in unison. It was Alhaji's private joke, a play on the first syllables of their names. They no longer found it funny but knew better than not to humour the patient, a longstanding one at that, who happened to be one of the richest men in the world.

Alhaji doubted that anger had anything to do with his blood pressure. If only he could curb his fondness for putting salt in everything, he was sure all would be well. Whatever anyone else said—even if they were two of the most eminent physicians in their field—Alhaji always made up his own mind. There was something about billionaires and that kind of stubborn self-belief.

"Aargh, Alhaji is singing, which means that his own contribution is a sure banker?"

Alhaji took off his Panthere glasses, put them in their crocodile skin case and composed himself. Even if he believed that anger had nothing to do with hypertension, he was taking no chances.

"With due respect, Mr. President, you must be out of your mind."

To say that His Excellency, President Aremu Oladipo, commander-in-chief of the armed forces and grand commander of the order of the federation, was taken aback would be to indulge in understatement. But he too was an expert at masking anger. You did not get to become leader of the world's most querulous people without knowing how to take an insult.

"Ah-ah, Alhaji, I beg your pardon—there is no need for such language now."

"No, I beg *your* pardon, Mr. President." Alhaji's voice was rising. "Why should I contribute even one kobo, not to talk of millions of dollars, to that lackey?"

Because I, the president, say so, the president thought, but he did not utter the words. Instead, he smiled broadly. It was the practiced smile that had charmed a nation into electing him, twice. Regrettably, it had not been enough to get them to change the constitution to give him a third term.

Yes, the candidate he was pushing to succeed him was a lackey but so what? That was why he wanted the man. The next best thing to running was to put up someone he could control. He would become the master puppeteer, pulling strings from the wings, as chairman of the party's board of trustees.

The president made a mental note to check with the director of state security on arresting Dr. Ken Onovo. The Senate President's renowned eloquence had been put to the wrong use on the floor of the National Assembly to destroy the "third-term project." Just desserts were therefore due to the politician from the Southeast who would soon learn that the child who caused his mother not to sleep was thereby condemned to sleeplessness as well.

The president considered himself quite the magnanimous person in ordinary life, but this was politics. If the next man took one of your eyes, you made sure to take both of his. And those of his family. And of his friends. You smote his lineage and scattered their ashes so that others would know you had no cheek to turn, and not dare, even in their wildest imagination, to cross you.

"Ah-ah, Alhaji, cool down, it will work out for you and for all of us," the president laughed, returning his attention to matters at hand. "He will be elected, and he will do our bidding, trust me."

"That buffoon will do you and whose bidding, Mr. President?" Alhaji had somehow got his voice back under control. "I'm sorry but I cannot be a part of this charade."

Alhaji Sani looked around him for support. The president had gathered the richest businessmen in the country—"captains of industry," they were called. There were no aides in the chamber; it was that kind of meeting. Only the president and the big men gathered around the table would be able to speak to what had transpired in the room, which meant that no one would.

Alhaji Sani wondered how anyone in his right mind would consider Fortuna Johnson a sellable candidate. The man was an electoral disaster waiting to happen, even if, as usual, the vote would be rigged. This was, after all, a man whom *The Economist* had called a "wimp" and the *WSJ* "clueless." He could not be counted on to win an election in his hometown, talk less of the national polls.

Alhaji had come, therefore, expecting robust dialogue on the Johnson candidacy and perhaps agreement on someone more credible. Instead, after pleasantries, the president began announcing donations that he, the president, in his infinite wisdom, had decided on behalf of each of the men gathered here.

"Tony, yours is ten million." This was to Anthony Eluemuno, chairman and controlling shareholder of Africa United Bank, who was also heavily invested in hotels and food processing plants.

"Mike, yours is fifteen million." Michael Adeniyi Jr. was the owner of Shine, the biggest phone company in the country, and several oilfields.

"Armani will just give us twelve million." Orji Nnamani or "Armani" as he liked to be called. A jack of many trades, including shipping and media, Orji had gone into business in his early twenties after rustication from university for leading violent student demonstrations. He never got the degree but the vice-chancellor who'd signed his expulsion papers now worked for him as general manager.

And so it went around the room, until the president had tallied an election war chest that would put many small countries' budgets to shame.

There was a glossy folder marked "Health-is-Wealth Foundation" on the table in front of each man. The president did not talk about the folder, and his invitees did not ask, but everybody understood why it was there. Inside was a single sheet of paper bearing the details of the foundation's bank account.

The president announced Alhaji Sani's donation last. It was to be the biggest contribution. Alhaji did not quarrel with that. He was richer than everybody in the room put together, and they knew it. His problem was with the president's double imposition.

Surely, the president would have had the courtesy to consult with each of them first? They had all donated handsomely to his elections. The first time, he'd come literally cap in hand. Alhaji remembered him sitting at the edge of the chair in Alhaji's penthouse office on Sani Towers, answering "yes, sir" to everything. Now, eight years later, he was full of audacity. Alhaji shook his head. Politicians were all the same—a little time in office and they started to think that after God, it was them.

Alhaji Sani had expected others here to back him and pour sand into the president's *garri*. Money was power after all. With the vast fortunes at their disposal, they could combine enough to bring down any government.

"Who else is coming?" Alhaji had asked when Dr. Abdul, the president's chief of staff, had called with the invitation. Abdul coughed, hesitating, but Alhaji insisted. "My friend, talk now or I'll call the president myself." Abdul garbled the names, and it was a roll call of the country's richest. Alhaji was hardly surprised. Party primaries were a mere two months away.

Sitting across the table was Alhaji Inuwa. The military contractor and international arms dealer had just donated seven million dollars to Caltech, where seven of his nineteen children had taken their degrees. Inuwa was known to be a no-nonsense fellow. Today, he had simply nodded when the president requested him to "do the same as you did for the Americans, but for a more worthy cause."

Alhaji Sani glared at Inuwa, but the latter responded with a shrug.

Alhaji Sani then tried to make eye contact with Orji, from whom Alhaji had expected a typically hotheaded response. The Armani-clad university dropout stared into space.

Realising it was up to him alone, Alhaji cleared his throat. Immediately, he felt a dig under the table. It was Chris Senibo, physician to the president. The popular narrative was that the doctor of internal medicine had been rewarded for his professional services with fat bank accounts in Dubai. Alhaji knew the true story. Senibo was the first family's front for laundering their money into the Belizes and Panamas of this world.

Alhaji made to speak again but received an even sharper nudge. He decided he'd had enough. "With all due respect Your Excellency, I don't know if there is anything else Mr. President would like to discuss."

It was a breach of protocol bordering on an insult. Alhaji knew it, the president knew it and the rest of the people in the room knew it. Still, the president's visage wasn't broken.

"Chai, Alhaji, is that how it has reached?" The toothpaste smile. "You don't even have time for poor people like us again?"

Nervous laughter rippled around the table.

"No, Mr. President, it is not like that." Alhaji knew when to back down; his point was made. "I am just concerned that we might be keeping you from other important matters of state."

"You're quite right, Alhaji," the president conceded. "As always, I thank you for your kind consideration."

The president also knew how to stop people from stealing his thunder. Still smiling grandly, he stood up and went round the table to shake hands with each man, all of them having scrambled up as soon as he rose.

When the president got to Alhaji, he said, "Don't worry about it, Alhaji, we'll find another way to make up your share." Before Alhaji could think of a reply, the president had moved on to the man after to him. Oba Odubekun, construction, real estate and flour mills, a former chairman of the stock exchange, bowed low as the president shook with him.

And then the president was gone, departing in a flourish of flowing robes through the ornate door with the coat of arms which had opened automatically as he approached it.

Alhaji did not waste time with the backslapping and ribaldry that the group broke out into. He picked up the folder on the table and headed for the door opposite that through which the president had withdrawn.

"Ah-ah, Alhaji, you won't even greet your brother?"

Iniobong Etteh had stepped into his path, arms outstretched. Alhaji brushed past him. He had little regard for Etteh ordinarily, and more so now. The man's claim to fame was the giant oilfield he had assigned to himself, through a sham Mauritius company, during his time as minister of petroleum. The billion dollars that a Russian oligarch subsequently paid for the company was what had given Etteh a place at the table today.

Alhaji did not like people who became rich from public office. "The money to respect," he often told his aides, "is the money steeped in the sweat of your brow."

He admired only entrepreneurs like Inuwa and Orji who, like him, had thrived in the cut-throat world of business. True, Orji had done a term as state governor and had plundered the treasury as was the fashion, but he could be forgiven. He'd been certifiably rich before he ran for office. The same could not be said of Etteh, a petroleum economist of modest means prior to being plucked from obscurity by his former classmate of a president.

A multitude of aides, clutching phones and walkie-talkies, were waiting outside for their affluent patrons. They all jumped up as the door opened and Alhaji strode out. Aliko, Alhaji's nephew and personal assistant, rushed to him and took the folder, handing over Alhaji's diamond encrusted GoldVish phones.

As Alhaji checked to see who had called him, Aliko barked instructions over a two-way radio.

Heading for the airport in his convoy of black stretch SUVs, Alhaji pored over the latest *Forbes* Billionaires issue—anything to take his mind off the vexatious events at the Villa. He was still the richest man in Africa. It thrilled him to have once again surpassed Dangote, Oppenheimer and Sawiris. He was even up a few places on the global list.

"Aha," he told Aliko when the assistant first handed the magazine to him, "it is with cement that I have cemented my position on this list."

Alhaji had laughed at his own pun, wondering how he could use it with Selwyn and Ahmed next time he saw them. For years, he had been the only one who could import cement into the country.

"Cement?" the then president Magaji had queried. There would be two presidents after Magaji before the current oaf, Oladipo, was elected.

"Yes, cement," Alhaji had echoed. "Just trust me."

Alhaji was Magaji's sole supporter of means when the unfancied tailor from Kano, perennially in dark glasses, had decided to run for the state assembly. Defying the odds, Alhaji's money ensured not only that Magaji won but that he became speaker and then went on to national prominence as a senator before vying for president. When Magaji was swept into the Villa by a landslide, Alhaji presented his demand.

"I do not understand, Alhaji, *gaskiya,* but your wish is my command."

Anyone else would have asked for an oil license. Not Alhaji. He was more interested in the construction boom that oil was fueling. The more the cranes went up, the more prized cement became. But only the hardiest entrepreneurs could deal in it on a grand scale. Even smugglers had no appetite for something so heavy which had to be kept dry always.

Alhaji's business was uniquely positioned. His fleet of trucks had become the largest in the land to distribute yet another commodity that needed careful handling. A previous president, in similar circumstances as Magaji, had signed the customs order making Alhaji the only person who could import sugar.

"*Kai,* this thing is a no-brainer," Alhaji told his bemused executives. "Once we corner cement too, it will be like we are printing our own money."

Cement was also the foundation of Alhaji's friendship with Oba Odubekun, him of the recurrent "Alhaji, give me discount, abeg." Alhaji never failed to oblige, and Odubekun never failed to outbid his rivals for the biggest construction projects. If that didn't count for something in situations like today's, perhaps it was time to reconsider the discounts. How did they say it? Do me, I do you, God no go vex. Alhaji grunted.

His thoughts drifted more affectionately to Chief "Father-father" Kalu, the granddaddy of all movers and shakers. Father-father's success in cornering the stockfish market and becoming the original *mutumin mai kudi*—god of fat money—in the country, had convinced a precocious young Alhaji that controlling the trade in something consumed every day was the way to go.

How Alhaji would have loved the phlegmatic chief to have been at today's meeting. Alas, the old man was now too frail to travel, even if he still cast an iron hand over stockfish from his "small London" country home.

As the convoy swept into the airport, heading towards his gleaming Gulfstream, Alhaji noticed something wrong. His usually unflappable Israeli captain, Lev Aaronovitch, was standing at the foot of the plane, furiously mopping his brow. The captain's shirt was untucked and his tie was askew.

"Shalom, Alhaji," Aaronovitch said, as Aliko opened the door of the SUV for Alhaji.

"Shalom, Lev," Alhaji responded. "For an African, you are looking very white."

It was another of Alhaji's stock jokes, in use since he had got the government to issue a passport, by presidential decree no less, to Aaronovitch. Normally, Aaronovitch laughed. Now he did not.

"Sir, immigration just left the plane."

"What?" Alhaji thundered, in disbelief. "How can?"

Aaronovitch explained that armed immigration officers had ransacked the plane and impounded the Israeli crew's passports. When Aaronovitch protested, their leader pointed a gun in his face and sneered, "My friend, be very careful, you want us to give you your passport and arrest you instead?"

Alhaji Sani was stunned. The billionaire's premises and property were off-limits to any kind of law enforcement. Everybody knew that. The heads of police, customs and immigration were all his "boys," having been nominated by him. They also happened to be the beneficiaries of numbered Swiss accounts generously funded by the Sani Group. Alhaji called the comptroller general of immigration.

Bugaje answered on the first ring. "Yes, sir, Alhaji, sir, your boy is very loyal."

"Why did your men enter my plane?" Alhaji was curt.

"Wha-what do you mean, sir?"

"Bugaje, look, don't be stupid," Alhaji was struggling to restrain himself. "Immigration boarded my plane just now and harassed my people and you're asking me what I mean?"

"What? So-so-sorry, sir, but I don't..." came the strangled reply.

"You don't what, Bugaje?"

"To God who made me, sir, I don't know anything about it." Bugaje sounded genuinely confused. And petrified.

"Well, it happened, and I want to know why immediately!" Despite himself, Alhaji was shouting.

"Allah *ya kiyaye*, sir." Bugaje's voice was ghostly. "I take God beg you, I will send a signal to all formations immediately and find out."

"If you value your job, you better call me back at once, you hear me?" Alhaji ended the call before Bugaje could reply.

Alhaji got on the plane and asked Aaronovitch to keep the engines running while he waited for Bugaje's call. He was flying to Lagos for a ceremony the next day that promised to be momentous even by his standards. No one in the country had ever received, at a go, the number of cargoes of sugar and cement to be discharged at the port for the Sani Group.

The ambassadors of China and Brazil, where the shipments came from, would be at Apapa with him, as would the vice-president and a constellation of other dignitaries. Saturation coverage from local and international media was assured—his PR team had "seen" the chief correspondents in customary fashion.

A sizeable crowd of market women, trade unionists and students had also been rented to sing Alhaji's praises at the event. A bit of vulgarity every now and then was permissible, Alhaji mused, if nothing else to remind everyone, high and low, who was still the money god of all money gods.

Ten minutes later, as Alhaji tucked into some heavily salted *kilishi* strips that his crew had rustled up to calm their boss, Aliko nervously brought the phone to Alhaji.

"Sir, it is Joe."

Joseph Makanujola, CEO, Sani Cement.

"What does he want?" queried Alhaji, tugging at some *kilishi*.

"Erm, he wants to speak to you directly, sir." Aliko thrust the phone forwards, shaking it to indicate urgency.

Alhaji glared at him but wiped his hands on an SG-monogrammed napkin and took the phone. "Yes, Joe, what is it?"

"Sir, customs and navy have just boarded the vessels."

"Which vessels?" Alhaji asked, his voice rising.

"The ones carrying the sugar and the cement," came the reply. "They say they are impounding them to search for contraband."

Alhaji was quiet for a moment. Rather than interfere, the navy always escorted Sani's ships into port to make sure they were given priority berths. The head of the navy was another of his boys. Once the ships docked, customs fast-tracked clearance so that offloading could be completed within hours. No Sani cargo had ever been stopped or delayed.

"Did you talk to the chief of naval staff?"

"Yes, sir," Joe answered.

"And?"

"He says he doesn't know anything about it."

Joe was expecting an explosion and braced himself, but none came. Instead, Alhaji Sani's voice on the other end of the line became rather normal, pleasant even.

"Hmmm, okay o. And what about the comptroller general of customs?" Alhaji asked.

"His phones are switched off, sir."

Alhaji smiled to himself. "Okay, Joe, stay on it while I make a few calls myself."

Alhaji handed back the phone to Aliko and resumed his battle with the *kilishi*. He took his time to polish off the very last of the dried meat and then drank some orange juice, gazing out of the window at passenger airliners landing some distance away in the adjoining public airport. It had been over twenty years since he'd set foot on a commercial flight, but he was still certain that the orange juice on his jets tasted better than the juice in first class. Fate had been kind to him. But that was because he had learnt to be the master of his own fate.

Alhaji asked Aliko for one of his phones. As soon as the GoldVish was in his hands, he punched a number.

"Hello, Alhaji, sir," the managing director of Africa United Bank answered. "This one that you are calling personally, sir, I hope no problem?"

"I want an urgent transfer."

"Oh okay, sir, what amount and to what account?"

"Aliko will give you the details," Alhaji said. "It is to an organisation called Health-is-Wealth Foundation."

"Ah, okay, sir, understood," came the bright reply. "Consider it done."

Alhaji handed the phone to Aliko and resumed his gazing out of the window, a wry grin on his face.

POLICE IS YOUR
FRIEND

He knew the two men were police detectives immediately as he saw them. Why did policemen always stand out like that? Even when they tried to be in mufti like these two, you could spot them from a mile off. At least, the man knew he could. Perhaps it was the "police look" on their faces, perennially menacing, even when they smiled. Or maybe it was their clothes. Whatever it was, the man could tell a policeman, even in a crowded marketplace.

The taller of the two had on a faded, blue polo shirt, buttoned at the collar. The shirt was tucked into his trousers which he had pulled up to his stomach. This was another giveaway. Only police or Alaba traders wore their trousers this way. To make matters worse, the trousers were pleated—who but policemen still had pleats when all the rage was flat fronts?

The other one was short and stocky, dressed in traditional attire. His sleeveless *buba* top did little to hide his protruding belly. The *sokoto* trousers were too tight and rode up the insides of his thighs, giving him a k-legged appearance. Both had the shiny faces of people who worked too much in the sun or in places without air conditioning.

The man was sitting on the dwarf wall which formed the perimeter of a compound with two blocks of flats. He saw the policemen looking inquiringly at the buildings as they approached. When they were abreast of him, they stopped.

"Bros," the taller one said, "good afternoon o."

"Good afternoon, OC," the man answered. "Any better?"

"No better, my brother," the policeman answered, seeming unperturbed that the stranger recognised them as police on sight—hence his usage of "OC," for officer in charge. "You live here?"

"Yes o," the man responded.

"There is somebody like that who we are looking for," the shorter one said.

"Who he be?" the man enquired.

The tall policeman glanced into the loose-leaf file he carried. The tattered folder bore the initials of the criminal investigation department. "They say his name is Parker Okeke, alias Parker Pen."

The man frowned and looked back towards the block of flats.

"If it is the man I am thinking of, his flat is inside that block," said the man, pointing to the building on the left of the gate. "What car is he driving?"

"Nobody told us that one," the stocky policeman responded.

"Okay," the man said, getting down from the wall to stand by the policemen. "Perhaps you can check that place I told you."

The two policemen thanked him and headed into the premises. Watching them until they entered the block of flats he had pointed them to, Parker "Pen" Okeke then walked casually across the road to his car, started it and drove off.

Shortly after eight o'clock that night, Parker knocked on the door of the flat in Dolphin Estate. Dolphin was originally built as a luxury tenement but had since deteriorated into something of a ghetto from overcrowding and poor maintenance. However, the people that lived here still considered themselves middle class, including the assistant commissioner of police, or ACP for short, whom Parker came to see.

"Ah, *oga* Parker, welcome, sir," the houseboy said, full of smiles as he ushered in the regular visitor. "My master is on the table."

Parker walked past the tiny foyer into the living room. There on the settee, hunched over a stool bearing a mound of pounded yam and *orishirishi*-filled okra soup, was ACP Agbu.

"Parker, Parker, Parker Pen, you meet me well!" the ACP exclaimed, mouth full of food. "Wash hand and join me—food plenty."

Ordinarily, Parker would have taken up the invitation even if he weren't hungry. There was nothing that created more bonding between men than sharing a meal, especially when it was fare that was consumed with the hands. This evening though, Parker had come for serious business. He politely declined the offer and settled into the chair opposite the ACP.

"This one you're not eating, I hope all is well," the ACP said as he took a chunk of meat from the soup.

"No, sir, there is a problem."

"Ah-ah, what happened again?"

"Sir, just finish eating first," Parker said, even though he was itching to speak.

"See this man o, are you a stranger in this house?" the ACP enquired, chewing on another piece of meat. "Talk, *boh*!"

Parker didn't need a second telling and narrated his encounter with the policemen.

The ACP didn't stop eating but nodded intermittently to show attentiveness. "And what makes you think that it was you that they were looking for?"

"*Oga*, I say they called my name," Parker protested. "They even said 'Parker Pen.'"

"Ah, okay, it was you then." Another mouthful of pounded yam. "Can you describe them?"

Parker delivered his best recollection of the men, his mind going to the Laurel and Hardy movies that he'd watched as a child. He doubted that this ACP would have even the foggiest idea of who the comedians were. But Agbu could certainly hazard the policemen that came looking for Parker. Agbu commanded the special fraud unit at the FCID.

"It is looking as if it is Gromyko and Tallest o," Agbu said. "They are handling plenty 419 petitions these days."

"*Oga*, I don't need that kind of trouble o," Parker pleaded. "I have better-better jobs I have been working on since that my *mugu*—sorry, my client, sir—is about to pay."

"So you don't want police to be dragging you up and down all over the place now?" The ACP grinned at Parker and raised his eyebrows twice in quick succession.

Parker knew the cue. He put his hands in his pocket and brought out an envelope whose wad-like shape left no doubt about what it contained. He placed the envelope beside the tray of fufu from where it was deftly picked up by the ACP and stuffed into the side of the sofa.

"Ah, Parker, Parker, I trust," the ACP beamed. "I will tell you what to do, but meanwhile, abeg, let this boy bring you lager."

Early the next morning, Parker arrived at the FCID headquarters and inquired of the investigating police officer called Salisu.

"I don't know if Tallest is around, but I saw his second just now," said the policewoman at the counter. "Take seat, let me call him."

He watched the woman's ample backside recede into the inner recesses of the building and wondered if Agbu had dallied with her before. The ACP he knew was passionate about food, women and dollar bills, although not necessarily in that order. Parker made a mental note to ask Agbu about her later.

The policewoman returned shortly with the stocky man that was one half of the duo he had encountered the day before. "Gromyko," the woman introduced, "this is the man finding Tallest."

Parker stood up from the concrete bench and shook Gromyko's proffered hand. The policeman squinted momentarily as if trying to recollect where he'd seen Parker before. Good luck with that, thought Parker, cocksure that his dark suit and tie would throw Gromyko off. The man they'd met by the wall yesterday had been dressed in shorts, T-shirt and baseball cap turned backwards. This one looked every inch a lawyer.

"Good afternoon, sir," Gromyko said in a deferential tone, bowing slightly. "What can we do for you?"

"I was informed you were looking for me," Parker answered solemnly. "My name is Parker Okeke."

The policeman's eyes narrowed again immediately. "Oh, you are the one they call Parker Pen?" Stripped of deference, his voice now veered towards contempt. "But wait *sef*—is it not you that we saw yesterday?"

Parker maintained his air of superiority. "No, I have never seen you before, officer."

"Ah, okay o," Gromyko said, sneering. Even if this was not the man they met yesterday, he was always pleased to bring down all these people who thought they were *oga patapata* because they had gone to school.

"And what is this about, officer, if I may ask?" Parker was determined to retain the high ground.

"*Oga*, it is not for me to say," Gromyko offered. "You will come and wait in the investigation room while I go to find Tallest."

Parker followed him to an office comprising two rows of wooden tables, each with benches on either side. He sat by the table nearest the door while Gromyko departed in search of his superior officer. There were two other people in the office, sitting at a table on the far end. The one whose face Parker could see was clearly a policeman, while the man opposite him was in a black suit like Parker's. He was probably a lawyer, Parker reflected, or someone like him, passing off.

The dark-suited man and the policeman were leaning across the table so that their heads were close to each other, talking in little more than whispers. Parker laughed inwardly. Police stations were theatres of perennial negotiation. He wondered whether it was a release or arrest they were bargaining over. Just then, the dark-suited man looked over his shoulder warily as if to check whether anyone was listening in. Sizing Parker up, he nodded almost imperceptibly.

Parker nodded back in acknowledgement and then made a show of averting his gaze to confirm that not only could he not possibly make out what they were saying but that he didn't really care. Looking out of the window, he surveyed the detritus of the police yard.

Rusting vehicle carcasses littered the place, some bearing the fast-fading colours of the police and others not, suggesting the latter were impounded from the public but never released. The ground, un-paved and untended, was covered in weeds, especially around a big, old tire in which had collected a murky pool. Two fly-ridden mongrels skulked around, foraging for morsels and dodging the occasional boot aimed in their direction.

Parker shook his head. It was a wonder that policemen could muster anything resembling good cheer in this kind of environment. He almost empathised but checked himself.

The conference going on across the room had evidently finished. The two participants gathered the papers that were spread on the table between them and, shaking hands, made to exit. As they passed by him, the policeman smiled in Parker's direction and said, "Counsel,

I greet o." Parker responded cheerily, feeling no guilt. He had the learning after all and, but for the small matter of Joe, would have had the certificate too.

"Excuse me, sir," the student next to Parker had called, raising his hand. Parker, scribbling away furiously, paid him no heed, assuming that it was an extra answer sheet being requested. Parker's astonishment knew no bounds when the invigilator came over and the Jehovah's Witness of a classmate announced loudly, "Sir, this boy here just brought out answer booklet from his trouser."

Parker was a chief proponent of Joe, unabashedly lecturing the uninitiated on its merits, once he'd had a few beers.

"For Small Joe, you get small pieces of paper and write down small-small notes on the topics you want to answer," he would explain. "But Big Joe is the highest; you jot the notes inside answer booklet and carry the booklet into the exam."

"But how can they not see you are carrying something?"

"Ah-ah, small thing," was Parker's condescending reply. "Small Joe is inside your pocket, but for Big Joe, you have to wrap it around your leg and hold it tight with your socks, under your trouser."

Parker had the grades to show for four years of Joe. He was comfortably in the running for a second-class upper degree with this being his last exam.

The expulsion that followed devastated Parker, especially as it meant that he would probably never be a lawyer. But it was then that he'd found his true calling, the one he soon realised he'd been born to pursue.

"Inspector, this is the Parker Pen o," Gromyko confirmed to Tallest, as the two IPOs walked into the room.

Parker stood up to shake hands.

"Ah, *oga*, sit down o," said Tallest, whose clothes were different from the day before. Placing a file on the table that was bulkier than the one he carried the day before, Tallest settled onto the bench across from Parker. When Gromyko made no move to sit, Parker knew he'd been assigned the "bad cop" role, as Americans called it. Good o, bad o, whichever way they were coming, he was ready for them.

"Let me just switch off my phone, Inspector," Parker said. He pressed send, deleted the sent message and switched off the phone. "Enh-henh, Inspector...?"

"It is 419 we are investigating, Mr. Parker," Tallest answered, smiling.

Of course, that would be what they were investigating. Why else would they be interested in Parker Pen if not for section 419 of the criminal code? Parker knew the section by heart: any person who by false pretenses induces another person to deliver anything capable of being stolen is guilty of an offence.

"And what has that got to do with me?" Parker queried, hoping his expression came across as stony-faced as he intended.

"Ah, it has plenty o to do with you, Mr. Parker," the IPO answered. "Every time, every time, 'it is Parker Pen that helped me to write it, it is Parker Pen that helped me to write it.'"

"I don't understand—write what?"

"Write 419 email," Gromyko bellowed, in character. "You be 419er. Stop pretending you are a responsible man."

Parker glanced at Gromyko quizzically and turned again to Tallest.

"All the job boys we catch in your area say it is you that writes email for them," Tallest explained. "You see this file? It is full of statements by *yahoo-yahoo* boys in that your area calling your name."

"Ah, sorry o, Inspector, I think there must be a mistake."

"Mistake? Which kind of dirty mistake is that?" Bad cop was doing his thing again. "You think police is foolish, *abi*? We will see who be proper foolish today."

Tallest looked at Gromyko as if to ask him to cool down, but Parker knew it was all part of the routine. The IPO continued in an even tone. "Sir, we want you to write statement."

"Statement? About what, exactly?"

"You will write statement about how you are a 419er," Gromyko said, thrusting a sheet of paper in front of Parker and slapping a ballpoint pen on it. Parker pushed aside the pen, put on his glasses and looked at the statement form. After the section for filling in personal details, there was a declaration to be signed by the maker, if he or she were an accused person, that a caution had been administered.

"So, am I an accused or a witness?" Parker inquired.

"Right now, sir, it will depend on what you tell us," Tallest replied.

Your Destiny Is Calling Business Center. The name had tickled Parker enough to make him go in on a whim to compose yet another appeal to the Council of Legal Education. Crowded around the screen in the booth next to his were a group of men about his age, talking and gesticulating animatedly. In short order, from casually inquiring about the cause of excitement to correcting the grammar in an email phishing for bank account information, Parker crossed the Rubicon into the world of 419 cyber scamming.

That had been four years ago. Now he was the go-to person in his circles for composing the emails most likely to "catch" around the world. His destiny had called indeed, and he'd sworn after the exam debacle that no busybody, not least of all the two *odeh*—blockheads— across from him now, was going to get in the way of his destiny again.

"Inspector, I am sorry to disappoint you, but I know nothing of what you are talking about."

"You say you know nothing? Nonsense! We will just arrest you now, and then you will know something by force."

Parker ignored Gromyko. He was humouring their routine by focusing on the policeman that seemed kindly. He was also confident that he could checkmate them better than most that they'd had in here for 419. "Do you have a warrant, Inspector?"

"Ah, you this man, you want to lawyer us now?" Tallest beamed.

Parker read the IPO's evasiveness to mean that there was no warrant. The code said that a person could not be arrested without warrant for a 419 offence except if he was caught in the act. Parker took comfort in that, but only just. He understood as well as anyone that IPOs often didn't care for the niceties. They could throw him in the cell for days and nothing more would happen to them than a judge telling them off in court. While their thinking him a lawyer would certainly make them more cautious, long gone were the days when policemen were afraid of confronting "learned men."

"Okay, let's make this simple, Inspector," Parker said, pretending to cooperate. "Ask me specifically what you want to know, and if it is something I know about, I will write the answer for you." As he spoke, Parker filled in his personal information on the form.

"Aha, now you are behaving like a gentleman," Gromyko said.

The inspector waited for Parker to finish writing before he commenced the questioning. "How do you know Jones? Jones Lawani?"

The Spiderman! Parker knew Jones well. He was called Spiderman because he had a web of contacts around the globe. Jones could make things happen with just one phone call, be it to manufacture a government certificate in Malaysia or open a bank account in Portland, Maine. But Jones could not write in English to save his life, so his sometime partnerships with Parker were of mutual benefit. Jones, Jones! What had he got himself into now?

"Who is he?"

"See this man o, you are pretending you don't know Spider?" Gromyko looked incredulous, or perhaps he was still just acting.

"That is the one you people call Spiderman now..." the inspector offered.

"I'm sorry, Inspector, I don't know what or who you're talking about."

The inspector smiled and looked in the file. Gromyko was pacing up and down behind the inspector as if rearing to be let off a leash. Parker knew that at this point, he would have been in danger of a serious beating if he were an armed robbery or kidnapping suspect. But 419 was not a violent crime and the victims were foreigners—nonentities, in other words. A slap here and another there was all a 419er might expect during interrogation, but Parker considered he would be spared even that, at least for now, because they thought he might be a lawyer.

"Okay, what about Barrister Fred Adibua?"

Parker spotted the trick question. Who did not know Adibua? He was revered in the pantheon of 419ers, achieving near-mythical status in the days before the Internet when letters of solicitation were sent by fax.

Adibua concocted grandiose schemes even by today's standards. While on bail for "selling" the national theatre, he auctioned off the international airport and national stadium before posing as governor of the central bank and holding meetings with unsuspecting *mugus* in the real governor's office. Despite his exploits and multiple arrests, he had never been convicted.

Adibua was as flamboyant as he was shrewd. His throwing bundles of dollars at parties changed the face of money spraying forever and inspired the likes of Udu Bunch, Raining Dollar and Bastard Money who then turned it into an art form. If Parker said he had not heard of Adibua, then the IPO might determine that he was not being truthful.

"I have heard of him—who hasn't?" Parker answered.

"And?"

"And nothing, Inspector." Parker was as confident in the honesty of his denial as he was in falsity of the earlier ones. "I have heard of him, but I have never met him."

"At all, at all?"

"At all, Inspector."

"*Oga*, this man is not writing o," Gromyko complained.

"Don't worry, if it is to write, he must write today."

As the inspector looked in the file again, Parker wondered for the umpteenth time why the police were bothering with 419ers. *Yahoo* boys were just looking for way to make ends meet in a society where the big men and women were thieving the common people blind. If he had his way, the police would concentrate their meagre resources on the ministers and governors looting the treasury like no man's business.

And 419ing was work, hard work, truth be told. You had to have your wits about you and spend days, if not weeks or months, sending endless emails before a *mugu* took the bait. Parker shook his head at the injustice of it all. *Oyibo* people were getting cleverer by the day, and stories had to be ever more inventive to get them to send money. Why the police cared about them, he would never know—after all the things *oyibo* had done and continued to do to the continent?

"Okay, do you know one white man called Richard. . .err. . .Blakely?" The inspector pronounced the surname as "Black-ee-lie."

"No, I don't know him." Parker was genuinely getting annoyed now. Did "Black-ee-lie" pay tax here? If the man saw this crude inspector and the even cruder Gromyko, would he not turn up his nose at them and laugh at what he would think an abysmal parody of the white man's police?

Parker knew Blakely well. He and Spiderman had taken more than forty thousand pounds from Blakely over a few weeks. The idiot had turned up at the airport hoping to rescue a woman who had been lured into the country, scammed of all her savings, left stranded and in debt, by 419ers.

The idea had been Spiderman's, the writing Parker's and the photograph of said woman a random one poached from the Internet. What made it work was Blakely's attitude. He was the most patronising *mugu* Parker had ever seen, believing that he could singlehandedly rescue an English rose in distress and teach these feckless, obnoxious natives a thing or two in the process.

"See, everything I ask, you don't know. So, what do you know at all?"

"I don't know all these people you are asking about, I'm sorry."

"What do you mean you don't know Blackeelie? The man wrote petition against Spiderman, and Spiderman said it is you that wrote all the emails."

Oh, so that was what this was about. Blakely had hung around long enough to contact the police. Parker struggled to remain expressionless, but he was enraged at Spiderman's folly. He had warned Spiderman not to go to the airport, but Spiderman couldn't resist, proclaiming "He have more pound, I can taking it." The reckless fool.

"Sorry, I can't help you there."

Parker could see that the inspector was getting frustrated. So far, so good. But he had to keep his guard up. As unsophisticated and illiterate in information technology as they were, these policemen still had experience and a native intelligence that could not be underestimated.

"You will tell me now that you don't know another white man by name Phil Scudamore too, abi?"

"Phil Scudamore? Ah, now you're talking. I know that one now."

Parker was gratified by the reaction of the policemen. Gromyko stopped in midstride and stared wide-eyed at him. Tallest sat up, leaning forwards eagerly. They were convinced they had made a breakthrough.

"Enh-henh! Tell us now, how you know him?"

Scudamore was Blakely's partner and an old Etonian like his paramour. Parker had been surprised to find out Blakely was gay, since he'd assumed up to then that Blakely's interest in "Diana Parkes" was romantic. He had switched the tone of the emails after that to prey on other emotions—Diana pleading desperately that her scammers held her captive in a hotel and were threatening to use her as a sex slave if she did not pay up the remaining amount they requested. Yes, he knew Scudamore, who Blakely had said was as outraged as him about those terrible rogues even thinking of laying their filthy hands on poor Diana.

"I know him. Is he not that defender for…Manchester United?"

Inspector and Sergeant were equally dumbstruck. Gromyko recovered first and leaned across the table to smack Parker across the top of the head. Parker had been hit harder by his mother when he came home late from school, having tarried to play football, and thought nothing of it then. But now he reacted like the best Premier League footballers, rocking backwards as if hit by a bullet and nearly toppling over. Steadying himself, he put one hand to his head and sprang up, remonstrating.

"Are you mad? Sergeant, I say have you gone mad? Why are you hitting me?"

"It is you that is mad! Idiot. You are taking police for fools."

"Who the hell do you think you are? Are you crazy?" Parker was shouting.

Gromyko matched him. "It is you who is craze. You hear me? It is only Inspector saving you here!"

Parker and Gromyko jabbed their fingers at each other as they swapped invective at the top of their voices. Inspector Salisu aka Tallest sat watching them, arms across his chest, the bemused spectator.

Suddenly, Gromyko reared back and snapped to attention. The inspector scrambled up from his seat and executed a similar motion, stamping his feet and stiffening his arms at his sides. Sensing a presence behind him, Parker spun around.

"See, what is going on here? Why are you people disturbing the whole place?" asked a stern looking ACP Agbu, resplendent in the full uniform of his rank. He glared at the three men.

"Sir, we are interrogating a 419 suspect, sir," said the inspector. Gromyko nodded vigorously in agreement.

"Who? This man here?" asked Agbu, turning to face Parker squarely. There was not the slightest hint of recognition on the ACP's face. Upon the inspector's grunted acknowledgement, Agbu glowered at the said suspect. The look in his eyes chilled Parker to the bone—the ACP looked like he could kill. Parker had never seen this Agbu before. With his gaze still fixed on Parker, Agbu asked, "So what is causing the commotion?"

Thinking it was a prompt, Parker began to speak. Instantly, he found out he'd made a big mistake.

"Mister man, sharrap!" Agbu thundered. "Am I talking to you? Where do you think you are? Are you a policeman? Come on, keep quiet!"

Parker swallowed his apologies. Out of the corner of his eye, he noticed Gromyko smirk.

"Inspector?"

"Sir, this man is a suspect called Parker Okeke, alias Parker Pen."

"And?"

"We have several petitions against him and his co-conspirators, sir, including that one, Jones Lawani, Spiderman, sir, that you said we should charge to court."

"And?"

"We brought this one here for interrogation and we were asking him question gently when he started shouting at Sergeant just like that. Just like that, sir."

Parker was enraged at the glib lie and wanted to protest, but the murderous look the ACP shot him made him change his mind.

"So, what information have you obtained from him so far?"

"Sir, he has given us his name and address but nothing else. He has refused to write anything more. Everything we ask him, he says he doesn't know."

"He doesn't know?"

"That is what he says, sir…" replied a visibly flustered Inspector.

"But you know he knows?" the ACP pressed, his words uttered slowly, ominously.

"Sir, it is like…the evidence…" Tallest sounded constipated.

"Look here, my friend, answer my question! You know he knows?"

"Yes, sir!"

The ACP reached down and pressed his fingertips on the statement sheet. He regarded it for a moment, then dramatically turned it around so that it faced the side of the table that Tallest and Gromyko were on. "You said you know?"

"Yes sir."

"Okay, since he said he doesn't know but you said you know, you will now write the statement for him."

"But sir…" Tallest's voice had become a whisper.

"But what, Inspector? What are you butting? You don't know how to write again?"

"I do, sir, it is just that… I'm sorry, sir… Please don't be offended, sir… You see, sir…"

"I don't see anything, Inspector. I don't see anything here except two policemen wasting their time, my time and this gentleman's time!

I've warned you people here before. Stop wasting government time. The man says he doesn't know anything. What are you still wasting government time for?

"I'm…we're sorry, sir"

"Come on, give this man bail immediately—I said immediately o—and then I want to see both of you in my office."

"Yes, sir!' Tallest and Gromyko stamped their feet in unison.

ACP Agbu glowered at Parker one more time and then turned on his heel and stalked off.

There was a long silence in the room before the three men exhaled. The officers sank to their seats, and Parker followed suit on his side of the table.

Gromyko broke the enforced ice. Reaching across the table, he pushed his finger against Parker's forehead. This time, it was a decidedly playful gesture, and the sergeant was grinning. "You this man, *sef.* Instead of telling us you have settled *oga*, you are just here wasting our time since!"

"He heard what *oga* said, *abi*?" Tallest chimed in, mimicking the ACP's tone. "Stop wasting government time!" He hastily craned his neck towards the door, in afterthought, to check whether the ACP was well and truly out of earshot.

"*Oga*, make him just settle us our own now, before I prepare the bail," Gromyko suggested to Tallest, who smiled broadly at Parker in turn.

"Parker, Parker, Parker Pen. Mister Parker Pen. You heard Sergeant. Perform for us *jare*. It is not only the big men you will be settling. It is us that need it more even."

Parker grinned. Reaching into the inside pocket of his jacket, he brought out a wad-shaped envelope and put it into the file that lay between him and the Inspector.

A GREAT GOAT

The meeting of the Alpha Tau Omega fraternity of the University on the Niger was called to order.

"Great men!"

"Great, great, great!" resonated through the hall.

You had to be a great man to have qualified for admission to the fraternity, and you were certified great by having been so admitted.

"I greet you all, great men," the Grand Liege continued.

Another round of "great" was loosed upon the hall.

"We are gathered here at short notice to discuss a matter of paramount importance."

The black-clad men with white ties all nodded sagely in acknowledgement, shoulders squared in what they considered appropriate poise for the dignified in mind and body.

"That matter, as you all know, concerns the goat which should have been the centerpiece of our yearly banquet."

"Yes, great, uh-huh."

"Despite our having found and contracted *aboki* of appropriate skill as could handle the requisite barbeque and despite there being only a few hours to the banquet, there is still no goat."

"Where is our goat? *Kedu* our goat?" The cry came from the back of the hall.

"Precisely," the Grand Liege said, looking in the direction of the query. "Where is our goat?"

"Yes, where is it?"

The Grand Liege furrowed his brow. "Did we not, at the last gathering, delegate to the Grand Scriptor the task of procuring the said goat for us?"

"Yes, we did, Great. We did."

More furrowing of the brow. "And did we not, in the presence of all great men gathered then, present to the Grand Scriptor in cash, the sum budgeted for the said procurement?"

"Yes, we did. We did o."

"May I therefore crave your indulgence, great men, to call on the Grand Scriptor to explain to us why there is yet no goat tethered to a grazing post for us to behold in advance of the imminent arrival of *aboki* with sharp knives to commence the process of barbequing."

Alozie Okezie, the Grand Scriptor, stood up and adjusted his tie. He was tall and fair, looking every inch an *ajebutter*—child of privilege—despite a vastly different reality. It was not the polish of a pampered upbringing that manifested in such fulsome looks. Rather, fate, as quirky as ever, had randomly decided to compensate the pecuniary sleight of hand by conferring a most striking visage.

The senior Mr. Okezie, reputed to have been even more handsome in his youth than Alozie, was a court janitor. His regular interactions with affluent lawyers had made him determined that his offspring would acquire the best education and transform the lineage from havenots to have-a-lots. He'd driven his two children to study hard from an early age, an endeavour which had so far been rewarded with the best of intended outcomes.

On the strength of exceptional grades, Alozie had gone to King's College, that most elite of boarding schools, on a federal government scholarship. With A1s in all his SSE subjects, Alozie easily repeated the scholarship feat for university. Relatively straitened circumstances at home thus negated for the most part, Alozie was duly admitted on account of his looks and renowned intelligence into the Alpha Tau Omega fraternity, where he had become, no less, the Grand Scriptor for the year.

"Great men," the handsome Scriptor began.

"Great, great, great," came the reply, although there was also muttering, from the back, of "where is our goat?"

If Alozie heard the muted protestations, he did not show it. Instead, he spoke up confidently. "A great man went to a great market in search of a great goat."

It was an opening worthy of the best Grand Scriptors, and the hall responded accordingly. "Say it, great! Say it!"

Alozie smiled broadly.

"Upon getting to the great market, your Grand Scriptor made his way to what he perceived to be a great merchant in great goats. This merchant was clearly of patrician bearing, despite his being attired in humble clothes suitable for the daily rigours of his trade."

The assemblage was loving the narration and responded cheerily once more.

Alozie cast his gaze around the room, smiled again and continued. "Great men must understand that getting to this point was no easy task for a great man—your Grand Scriptor had to overlook the aggressive jostling, noxious odours and general uncouthness of the hoi polloi whose habit it is to throng such markets across the land."

This time, there was not only vocal approval but applause. The Grand Scriptor was in full flow.

"In any event, after haggling with the said goat merchant, in a manner most auspicious and befitting of men of unimpeachable countenance, a fair bargain was struck."

Applause. Pounding on tables. Shouts of "Great, speak that English, *biko*! Fire on!"

"Thus did I hand over to this merchant the great money which great men had aggregated for purposes of an ennobled purchase. To consummate the transaction, the merchant in turn handed over, at the end of a sturdy length of Indian hemp rope, a he-goat of the most magnificent proportions, sporting a mane as immaculate as if it had been polished by the gods themselves."

"Great, you done win! See English."

Up to this point, the Grand Scriptor had been a picture of amiability, but his face now turned serious, and his tone took on an urgency.

"Thereupon great men, I made my way out of that great arena of traders and trading, onto the main road which I intended to cross in order to join a befitting means of conveyance back to the distinguished company of great men in this great citadel of learning."

"Yes, Great?"

"As I waited patiently for the cars to pass, being of such dignified composure and upright bearing as only great men can muster amid a surrounding chaos, guess what happened, great men?"

"What happened? Motor hit you?"

Pregnant pause.

"Ah-ah, talk now, Grand Scriptor?"

Alozie affected an expression of distaste before proceeding. "To my shock and amazement, great men, this goat, this outwardly magnificent specimen which I had assumed to be of patrician stock and expected to comport itself accordingly, revealed itself without warning to be a most contemptible plebeian. It suddenly broke loose of the rope and bolted into the congregating hordes which, as I earlier told you, were composed entirely of barbarians—save for me—as far as the eye could see."

"So? What exactly are you saying, Grand Scriptor?"

Alozie's voice now rose. "So, great men, I ask you, would any of you, in all good conscience, have deigned to descend into that abyss of the proletariat, abandoning all dignity and superior bearing to pursue this goat, now revealed to be a plebeian of the highest order, through the multitude of the unwashed and unlettered? Would any of you have taken that risk, to be identified as a plebeian rather than a great man? To drag the name of the Alpha Tau Omega in the mud, perhaps not only metaphorically but also literally, given the perilous state of the walkways following the rains that morning? Would you?"

"No, Grand Scriptor! How can? Of course not. *Tufiakwa!*"

Alozie smiled grandly now, revealing a brilliant set of white teeth. "Yes, of course not, great men. Your Grand Scriptor has sworn, like all of you, to always uphold the five letters of the Alpha, forswearing all distraction and resisting all temptation to the contrary, whatever they may be and wherever they may occur. It was, therefore, with a heavy heart at the loss of the goat but with immense pride at having lived up to the hallowed code of conduct of all great man who have gone before us and those who will come after, that I made my way back to campus to report the sad events which occurred as aforesaid."

There was an uncertain silence, but the Grand Scriptor moved quickly to fill it with his denouement. "In the circumstances, great men, I enquire—did your Grand Scriptor not acquit himself as creditably as any of you would have, given a similar turn of events? Did I not? I say unto you, did I not?

An outburst of approval greeted the rhetorical challenge.

"Yes of course, Great."

"You are truly a great man!"

"Great, great, great!"

"Great, if it is only for this English, *sef,* you done win!"

"Na you *biko*, Grand Scriptor!"

There were a few dissenting protestations of "*Bia nwokem*, you this man, where is our goat or *kedu* our money?" But they were swept aside as most of the great men rushed forwards to pump the Grand Scriptor's hand and pat him vigorously on the back.

And that was how it came to be that the twentieth annual banquet of the Alpha Tau Omega fraternity was conducted bereft of the traditional barbeque but otherwise in good cheer and dignified gaiety befitting of all great men, past and present, and those who were yet to come.

"Today is today," Mazi Enuke told Orie, his fourth and newest wife. "Today that son of a vulture will know who I am."

"But *nna anyi*," Orie implored, "Can't you just leave it?"

"Leave what? I say leave what? Someone is spoiling my name, and I should leave it? *Tufiakwa*. It won't happen."

"But everybody knows Mazi Amazu cannot be taken seriously."

"They *are* taking him seriously," Mazi Enuke replied. He put on his cap and looked at himself in the cracked mirror, a gift from Teacher Ikeji. At first, it was said that a mirror drove away one's *chi*, but now men of stature all had one, and he was glad for the good teacher's benevolence.

"*Nna anyi*, Mazi Obioha had many enemies," Orie said. "Any of them could have been the one that poisoned him."

"So why is Amazu pointing his dirty, stinking finger only at me?" Mazi Enuke was losing patience with his young wife. "I have to stop it now before it grows legs and then wings and flies like *Nduli* the bird to the ears of the Divisional Officer in Arochuku."

"But surely, DO cannot believe that kind of thing?"

"What do you know about what DO believes, Orie? How did all this start anyway?"

"The land...?"

"Yes, of course, the land," Enuke retorted. "It was the land."

"But DO said it belonged to them?"

"You see what I am saying? You see? What does DO know? That land has been in our family from when the world was created. My forefathers and their forefathers before them farmed that land."

"*Nna anyi*, don't be upset but Dei Uche said your Umunna has accepted the white man's decision, that after everything is said up and said down, it is just a small piece of land out of the many that the family has."

"I know, my *oriaku*, but that is why I am telling you that I don't trust that DO will believe anything as long as it is that thief of a *courtuma's* family that tells him."

Mazi Enuke grimaced. Yes, they had made their peace with DO's accursed decision, but what could they do? The world changed all of a sudden the day the white man arrived. Justice fled the land, displaced by the white man's strange dispensations with a force that even the gods were powerless against.

One did not have to look farther than at Okonkwo to know how far things had fallen apart. Okonkwo, a man for all seasons, a man among men. Okonkwo, the great wrestler, whose back had never touched the ground and who was reputed to have successfully grappled with his *chi* in the land of the spirits. The same Okonkwo had hanged himself rather than face the white man's justice.

And what had Okonkwo even done? He'd struck down the white man's messenger who dared desecrate the land. In the old days, when men were men, Okonkwo would have been feted and his legend multiplied beyond measure. But now? Mazi Enuke hissed. He would have spat but for the fact that Orie continuously berated him when he did so. She seemed to have learnt from the children who went to the white man's school that it was somehow wrong to do so. Mazi Enuke hissed again—one could not even spit in his own *iba* anymore without coming up against the white man's suffocating diktats.

Iheme's family had not even been part of the dispute. It had been the Diwe family that had challenged the ownership of the narrow strip of land running down to the Otamiri River out of which came the best yams for miles around. But Ahize, Iheme's since deceased son, had been the *courtuma*, the interpreter in the white man's court. Only God—Chukwu Abiama—and Ahize himself knew what Ahize had told the DO that day to make the DO declare that the land belonged to the Iheme family.

"But even the other white man said it belonged to the Iheme family as well?"

"Yes, when we realised what had happened, we sent emissaries to Aro, but upon getting there they were told that the one who pronounced that abomination of a judgment had gone back to their country."

"And the new one could not see the injustice?" Orie was puzzled—it was said the white man knew everything.

"No, he told us he could not change what had been written—that when it is written, it is written. That is how those *umu oru*, a lineage of servants, a people that are owned, came to own the most fertile piece of land in this village."

"But still, *nna anyi*..."

"Enough, Orie, enough!" Mazi Enuke exclaimed. "This useless talk is delaying me."

"I am sorry, *nna anyi*." Orie's voice was penitent. "Please forgive me."

Mazi Enuke softened. "No, Orie, there is nothing to forgive. You have spoken like a woman, like a good wife, but now I must act like a man should."

"I bid you well, *nna anyi*. May the ancestors guide your tongue before the elders."

Mazi Enuke smiled and touched her face gently. His fourth wife was young enough to be his daughter, but she spoke like she was his age-mate, like a man even. That precociousness was why he was so fond of her. But now there was business to be done. His face was set as he left the hut.

Amazu made a compelling case before the elders. He was the current *diokpa* of the Ihemes, following the canoe accident in which Ahize had drowned on the way to assizes with the DO. The white man was said to have swum like *Asa* the eel to the riverbank, but Ahize, for all his knowing the white man's ways, could only thrash about wildly until the Bonny River took him like it had taken many before him.

The gift of the gab ran through the many generations of the Iheme family. It was perhaps of little surprise that it had been one of them who had become the white man's first mouthpiece from the community. Only through an uncommon ability with words, even at an early age, had Ihemeukwu, their forebear, managed to escape the fate ordinarily reserved for "owned people" like him.

If only Okonkwo's beloved Ikemefuna had possessed the same talents. Perhaps he would similarly have talked his way out of being the offering the gods demanded, for the continued peace and progress of the community, as soon as he came of age. That sacrifice, inadvertently executed by Okonkwo in the heat of the moment, was perhaps the beginning of the great man's undoing. Everyone later said the gods were not happy that he whom the boy called "father" had struck the mortal blow in the confused circumstances of that sweltering *Afor* afternoon. Yes, indeed, the gods could be funny like that.

"Mazi Enuke, the elders await your response."

Jolted out of his reverie, Enuke scrambled up. "My elders, I greet you. I would have said I do not include Mazi Amazu in my greetings given the accusations he has levelled against me, but I greet him too, for our custom, the custom of our forefathers, demands it."

"Thank you, Mazi Enuke, for respecting the custom. You have heard the accusations?"

Yes, indeed he had heard the accusations, as well marshalled as they were. Amazu had been there when Enuke and Obioha jostled on the way from the farm. Obioha was Amazu's younger brother, a hardworking farmer to Amazu's perennial drunkard. Enuke had encountered Amazu sprawled by the footpath, inebriated and unable to get up. Contemplating Amazu with disgust, Enuke spat in his direction, not realising that Obioha had emerged from the bush on the other side of the path.

"*Anuofia*, you beast, why are you spitting on my brother?" Obioha had challenged.

"Look at him," Enuke countered. "Is he not deserving of even worse?"

Both men had squared up to each other and started to grapple. Luckily, a gaggle of other people heading to the farm came upon the scene and forced the two apart before any apparent damage was done. On the brothers' way from the encounter, however, Obioha complained repeatedly that Enuke had scratched him, wondering whether they needed to make a diversion to the *dibia* for remediating unguents, just in case. Enuke's family was renowned across all the Aros and beyond as possessing an outstanding knowledge of poisons and poisoning which had been passed down from generation to generation.

Two days later, Obioha and Amazu were preparing to set off for the farm when Obioha suddenly started drawling, his mouth curving downwards. He crumpled to the ground, unable to form words. Amazu thought he recognised this as what happened when a man had imbibed of too much palm wine from the *diochi*—he, Amazu, was better acquainted than most with the symptoms. The only problem was that Obioha never drank.

As Amazu dropped to his knees to cradle his brother's head, Obioha's body went into spasms, as if being struck at close range by unseen spirits. Amazu raised the alarm and other members of the kindred rushed out. Obioha was taken into his hut and made to drink water while the *dibia* was summoned.

The healer pronounced it a case of serious poisoning, but despite repeated visits over the next six weeks, could not remediate the problem. Obioha died on the seventh Orie day after he slumped, never speaking again or getting up from his bed.

Amazu had finished his declamation to the elders with a flourish. "And so, our elders, can it be said that it is a coincidence that my beloved brother, a picture of good health hitherto, was struck by a mysterious illness two days after his fight with Enuke and then died on Orie day—the same day for which Enuke's favourite wife is named? No, my elders, we say that if a witch cries at night and a child dies in the morning, we do not go to a soothsayer to ask what killed the child. Enuke must be reported to the DO and made to pay for my brother's murder."

Enuke knew he could not match the flowery language with which Amazu had presented. Nor did he intend to. He had his answer ready.

"My elders, you know my family. You know what we can do. I therefore ask you, if I decide to poison a man, do you think he will last a night, talk less of six Orie days? Think about it. My father's father was not acclaimed as Echieteka—tomorrow is too far—for nothing. If I had deigned to transmit a poison to that *nwanne* of theirs, he would be dead *piaaaa* before they reached their accursed kindred. Yes?"

The wizened old men looked around and acknowledged that no truer statement had been made that day. It would subsequently go down in legend that no quicker resolution had, in living memory, been reached in such a case. Even the loquacious Amazu was so taken by the logic of Enuke's statement that he had nothing to say when the elders asked him for a response. There would be no report made to the DO. Amazu and the rest of the Ihemes were bidden to cease and desist from further accusations against Enuke.

The triumphant scion of the family of poisoners majestically strode back to the comforts of Orie that night, pleased that not once had he lost his temper during that most provocative of trials.

Made in the USA
Columbia, SC
16 April 2022

59043756R00126